In Black and White by Rudyard Kipling

Rudyard Kipling: A great Victorian, a great writer of Empire, a great man.

Rudyard Kipling was one of the most popular writers of prose and poetry in the late 19th and 20th Century and awarded the Noble Prize for Literature in 1907.

Born in Bombay on 30th December 1865, as was the custom in those days, he and his sister were sent back to England when he was 5. The ill-treatment and cruelty by the couple who they boarded with in Portsmouth, Kipling himself suggested, contributed to the onset of his literary life. This was further enhanced by his return to India at age 16 to work on a local paper, as not only did this result in him writing constantly but also made him explore issues of identity and national allegiance which pervade much of his work.

Whilst he is best remembered for his classic children's stories and his popular poem 'If...' he is also regarded as a major innovator in the art of the short story.

Index of Contents

Dray Wara Yow Dee

Almonds and raisins, Sahib? Grapes from Kabul? Or a pony of the rarest if the Sahib will only come with me. He is thirteen-three, Sahib, plays polo, goes in a cart, carries a lady and—Holy Kurshed and the Blessed Imams, it is the Sahib himself! My heart is made fat and my eye glad. May you never be tired! As is cold water in the Tirah, so is the sight of a friend in a far place And what do you in this accursed land? South of Delhi, Sahib, you know the saying— 'Rats are the men and trulls the women.' It was an order? Ahoo! An order is an order till one is strong enough to disobey. O my brother, O my friend, we have met in an auspicious hour! Is all well in the heart and the body and the house? In a lucky day have we two come together again.

I am to go with you? Your favour is great. Will there be picket-room in the compound? I have three horses and the bundles and the horseboy. Moreover, remember that the police here hold me a horse-thief. What do these Lowland bastards know of horse-thieves? Do you remember that time in Peshawur when Kamal hammered on the gates of Jumrud—mountebank that he was—and lifted the Colonel's horses all in one night? Kamal is dead now, but his nephew has taken up the matter, and there will be more horses a-missing if the Khyber Levies do not look to it.

The Peace of God and the favour of His Prophet be upon this house and all that is in it I Shafiz Ullah, rope the mottled mare under the tree and draw water. The horses can stand in the sun, but double the felts over the loins. Nay, my friend, do not trouble to look them over. They are to sell to the Officer-fools who know so many things

2

of the horse. The mare is heavy in foal; the grey is a devil unlicked; and the dun—but you know the trick of the peg. When they are sold I go back to Pubbi, or, it may be, the Valley of Peshawur.

O friend of my heart, it is good to see you again. I have been bowing and lying all day to the Officer-Sahibs in respect to those horses; and my mouth is dry for straight talk. Auggrh! Before a meal tobacco is good. Do not join me, for we are not in our own country. Sit in the veranda and I will spread my cloth here. But first I will drink. In the name of God returning thanks, thrice! This is sweet water, indeed—sweet as the water of Sheoran when it comes from the snows.

They are all well and pleased in the North—Khoda Baksh and the others. Yar Khan has come down with the horses from Kurdistan—six-and thirty head only, and a full half pack-ponies—and has said openly in the Kashmir Serai that you English should send guns and blow the Amir into Hell. There are fifteen tolls now on the Kabul road; and at Dakka, when he thought he was clear, Yar Khan was stripped of all his Balkh stallions by the Governor! This is a great injustice, and Yar Khan is hot with rage. And of the others: Mahbub Ali is still at Pubbi, writing God knows what. Tugluq Khan is in jail for the business of the Kohat Police Post. Faiz Beg came down from Ismail-ki-Dhera with a Bokhariot belt for thee, my brother, at the closing of the year, but none knew whither thou hadst gone: there was no news left behind. The Cousins have taken a new run near Pakpattan to breed mules for the Government carts, and there is a story in the Bazar of a priest. Oho! Such a salt tale! Listen—

Sahib, why do you ask that? My clothes are fouled because of the dust on the road. My eyes are sad because of the glare of the sun. My feet are swollen because I have washed them in bitter water, and my cheeks are hollow because the food here is bad. Fire burn your money! What do I want with it? I am rich. I thought you were my friend. But you are like the others—a Sahib. Is a man sad? Give him money, say the Sahibs. Is he dishonoured? Give him money, say

3

the Sahibs. Hath he a wrong upon his head? Give him money, say the Sahibs. Such are the Sahibs, and such art thou—even thou.

Nay, do not look at the feet of the dun. Pity it is that I ever taught you to know the legs of a horse. Footsore? Be it so. What of that? The roads are hard. And the mare footsore? She bears a double burden, Sahib.

And now, I pray you, give me permission to depart. Great favour and honour has the Sahib done me, and graciously has he shown his belief that the horses are stolen. Will it please him to send me to the Thana? To call a sweeper and have me led away by one of these lizard-men? I am the Sahib's friend. I have drunk water in the shadow of his house, and he has blackened my face. Remains there anything more to do? Will the Sahib give me eight annas to make smooth the injury and—complete the insult—?

Forgive me, my brother. I knew not—I know not now—what I say. Yes, I lied to you! I will put dust on my head—and I am an Afridi! The horses have been marched footsore from the Valley to this place, and my eyes are dim, and my body aches for the want of sleep, and my heart is dried up with sorrow and shame. But as it was my shame, so by God the Dispenser of Justice—by Allah-al-Mumit!—it shall be my own revenge

We have spoken together with naked hearts before this, and our hands have dipped into the same dish, and thou hast been to me as a brother. Therefore I pay thee back with lies and ingratitude—as a Pathan. Listen now! When the grief of the soul is too heavy for endurance it may be a little eased by speech; and, moreover, the mind of a true man is as a well, and the pebble of confession dropped therein sinks and is no more seen. From the Valley have I come on foot, league by league, with a fire in my chest like the fire of the Pit. And why? Hast thou, then, so quickly forgotten our customs, among this folk who sell their wives and their daughters for silver? Come back with me to the North and be among men once more. Come back, when this matter is accomplished and I call for thee! The bloom of the peach-orchards is upon all the Valley, and here is only dust and a great stink. There is a pleasant wind among the mulberry trees, and the streams are bright with snow-water, and the caravans go up and the caravans go down, and a hundred fires sparkle in the gut of the Pass, and tent-peg answers hammer-nose, and pack-horse squeals to pack-horse across the drift-smoke of the evening. It is good in the North now. Come back with me. Let us return to our own people! Come.

Whence is my sorrow? Does a man tear out his heart and make fritters thereof over a slow fire for aught other than a woman? Do not laugh, friend of mine, for your time will also be. A woman of the Abazai was she, and I took her to wife to staunch the feud between our village and the men of Ghor. I am no longer young? The lime has touched my beard? True. I had no need of the wedding? Nay, but I loved her. What saith Rahman? 'Into whose heart Love enters, there is Folly and naught else. By a glance of the eye she hath blinded thee; and by the eyelids and the fringe of the eyelids taken thee into the captivity without ransom, and naught else.' Dost thou remember that song at the sheep-roasting in the Pindi camp among the Uzbegs of the Amir?

The Abazai are dogs and their women the servants of sin. There was a lover of her own people, but of that her father told me naught. My friend, curse for me in your prayers, as I curse at each praying from the Fakr to the Isha, the name of Daoud Shah, Abazai, whose head is still upon his neck, whose hands are still upon his wrists, who has done me dishonour, who has made my name a laughing-stock among the women of Little Malikand.

I went into Hindustan at the end of two months—to Cherat. I was gone twelve days only; but I had said that I would be fifteen days absent. This I did to try her, for it is written: 'Trust not the incapable.' Coming up the gorge alone in the falling of the light, I heard the voice of a man singing at the door of my house; and it was the voice of Daoud Shah, and the song that he sang was 'Dray wara yow dee'—'All three are one.' It was as though a heel-rope had been slipped round my heart and all the Devils were drawing it tight past endurance. I crept silently up the hill-road, but the fuse of my matchlock was wetted with the rain, and I could not slay Daoud Shah from afar. Moreover, it was in my mind to kill the woman also. Thus he sang, sitting outside my house, and, anon, the woman opened the door, and I came nearer, crawling on my belly among the rocks. I had only my to my hand. But a stone slipped under my foot, and the two looked down the hillside, and he, leaving his matchlock, fled from my anger, because he was afraid for the life that was in him. But the woman moved not till I stood in front of her, crying: 'O woman, what is this that thou hast done?' And she, void of fear, though she knew my thought, laughed, saying: 'It is a little thing. I loved him, and thou art a dog and cattlethief coming by night. Strike!' And I, being still blinded by her beauty, for, O my friend, the women of the Abazai are very fair, said: 'Hast thou no fear?' And she answered: 'None—but only the fear that I do not die.' Then said I 'Have no fear.' And she bowed her head, and I smote it off at the neck-bone so that it leaped between my feet. Thereafter the rage of our people came upon me, and I hacked off the breasts, that the men of Little Malikand might know the crime, and cast the body into the watercourse that flows to the Kabul River. Dray wara yow dee! Dray wara yow dee! The body without the head, the soul without light, and my own darkling heart—all three are one—all three are one!

That night, making no halt, I went to Ghor and demanded news of Daoud Shah. Men said 'He is gone to Pubbi for horses. What wouldst thou of him? There is peace between the villages.' I made answer: 'Ay! The peace of treachery and the love that the Devil Atala bore to Gurel.' So I fired thrice into the tower-gate and laughed and went my way.

In those hours, brother and friend of my heart's heart, the moon and the stars were as blood above me, and in my mouth was the taste of dry earth. Also, I broke no bread, and my drink was the rain of the valley of Ghor upon my face.

At Pubbi I found Mahbub Ali, the writer, sitting upon his charpoy, and gave up my arms according to your Law. But I was not grieved, for it was in my heart that I should kill Daoud Shah with my bare hands thus—as a man strips a bunch of raisins. Mahbub Ali said: 'Daoud Shah has even now gone hot-foot to Peshawur, and he will pick up his horses upon the road to Delhi, for it is said that the Bombay Tramway Company are buying horses there by the truckload; eight horses to the truck.' And that was a true saying.

Then I saw that the hunting would be no little thing, for the man was gone into your borders to save himself against my wrath. And shall he save himself so? Am I not alive? Though he run northward to the Dora and the snow, or southerly to the Black Water, I will follow him, as a lover follows the footsteps of his mistress, and coming upon him I will take him tenderly—Aho! so tenderly!—in my arms, saying: 'Well hast thou done and well shalt thou be repaid.' And out of that embrace Daoud Shah shall not go forth with the breath in his nostrils. Auggrh! Where is the pitcher? I am as thirsty as a mother mare in the first month.

Your Law! What is your Law to me? When the horses fight on the runs do they regard the boundary pillars; or do the kites of Ali Musjid forbear because the carrion lies under the shadow of the Ghor Kuttri? The matter began across the Border. It shall finish where God pleases. Here; in my own country; or in Hell. All three are one.

Listen now, sharer of the sorrow of my heart, and I will tell of the hunting. I followed to Peshawur from Pubbi, and I went to and fro about the streets of Peshawur like a houseless dog, seeking for my enemy. Once I thought that I saw him washing his mouth in the conduit in the big square, but when I came up he was gone. It may be that it was he, and, seeing my face, he had fled.

A girl of the bazar said that he would go to Nowshera. I said: 'O heart's heart, does Daoud Shah visit thee?' And she said: 'Even so.' I said: 'I would fain see him, for we be friends parted for two years. Hide me, I pray, here in the shadow of the window-shutter, and I will wait for his coming.' And the girl said: 'O Pathan, look into my eyes! ' And I turned, leaning upon her breast, and looked into her eyes, swearing that I spoke the very Truth of God. But she answered 'Never friend waited friend with such eyes. Lie to God and the Prophet, but to a woman ye cannot lie. Get hence! There shall no harm befall Daoud Shah by cause of me.'

I would have strangled that girl but for the fear of your Police; and thus the hunting would have come to naught. Therefore I only laughed and departed, and she leaned over the window-bar in the night and mocked me down the street. Her name is Jamun. When I have made my account with the man I will return to Peshawur and—her lovers shall desire her no more for her beauty's sake. She shall not be Jamun, but Ak, the cripple among trees. Ho! ho! Ak shall she be!

At Peshawur I bought the horses and grapes, and the almonds and dried fruits, that the reason of my wanderings might be open to the Government, and that there might be no hindrance upon the road. But when I came to Nowshera he was gone; and I knew not where to go. I stayed one day at Nowshera, and in the night a Voice spoke in my ears as I slept among the horses. All night it flew round my head and would not cease from whispering. I was upon my belly, sleeping as the Devils sleep, and it may have been that the Voice was the voice of a Devil. It said: 'Go south, and thou shalt come upon Daoud Shah.' Listen, my brother and chiefest among friends— listen! Is the tale a long one? Think how it was long to me. I have trodden every league of the road from Pubbi to this place; and from Nowshera my guide was only the Voice and the lust of vengeance.

To the Uttock I went, but that was no hindrance to me. Ho! ho! A man may turn the word twice, even in his trouble. The Uttock was no uttock [obstacle] to me; and I heard the Voice above the noise of the waters beating on the big rock, saying: 'Go to the right.' So I went to Pindigheb, and in those days my sleep was taken from me utterly, and the head of the woman of the Abazai was before me night and day, even as it had fallen between my feet. Dray wara yow dee! Dray wara yow dee! Fire, ashes, and my couch, all three are one—all three are one!

Now I was far from the winter path of the dealers who had gone to Sialkot, and so south by the rail and the Big Road to the line of cantonments; but there was a Sahib in camp at Pindigheb who bought from me a white mare at a good price, and told me that one Daoud Shah had passed to Shahpur with horses. Then I saw that the warning of the Voice was true, and made swift to come to the Salt Hills. The Jhelum was in flood, but I could not wait, and, in the crossing, a bay stallion was washed down and drowned. Herein was God hard to me—not in respect of the beast, of that I had no care— but in this snatching. While I was upon the right bank urging the horses into the water, Daoud Shah was upon the left; for—Alghias! Alghias!—the hoofs of my mare scattered the hot ashes of his fires when we came up the hither bank in the light of morning. But he had fled. His feet were made swift by the terror of Death. And I went south from Shahpur as the kite flies. I dared not turn aside lest I should miss my vengeance—which is my right. From Shahpur I skirted by the Jhelum, for I thought that he would avoid the Desert of the Rechna. But, presently, at Sahiwal, I turned away upon the road to Jhang, Samundri, and Gugera, till, upon a night, the mottled mare breasted the fence of the rail that runs to Montgomery. And that place was Okara, and the head of the woman of the Abazai lay upon the sand between my feet.

Thence I went to Fazilka, and they said that I was mad to bring starved horses there. The Voice was with me, and I was not mad, but only wearied, because I could not find Daoud Shah. It was written that I should not find him at Rania nor Bahadurgarh, and I came into Delhi from the west, and there also I found him not. My friend, I have seen many strange things in my wanderings. I have seen the Devils rioting across the Rechna as the stallions riot in spring. I have heard the Djinns calling to each other from holes in the sand, and I have seen them pass before my face. There are no Devils, say the Sahibs? They are very wise, but they do not know all things about Devils or—horses. Ho! ho! I say to you who are laughing at my misery, that I have seen the Devils at high noon whooping and leaping on the shoals of the Chenab. And was I afraid? My brother, when the desire of a man is set upon one thing alone, he fears neither God nor Man nor Devil. If my vengeance failed, I would splinter the Gates of Paradise with the butt of my gun, or I would cut my way into Hell with my knife, and I would call upon Those who Govern there for the body of Daoud Shah. What love so deep as hate?

Do not speak. I know the thought in your heart. Is the white of this eye clouded? How does the blood beat at the wrist? There is no madness in my flesh, but only the vehemence of the desire that has eaten me up. Listen!

South of Delhi I knew not the country at all. Therefore I cannot say where I went, but I passed through many cities. I knew only that it was laid upon me to go south. When the horses could march no more, I threw myself upon the earth and waited till the day. There was no sleep with me in that journeying; and that was a heavy burden. Dost thou know, brother of mine, the evil of wakefulness that cannot break—when the bones are sore for lack of sleep, and the skin of the temples twitches with weariness, and yet—there is no sleep—there is no sleep? Dray wara yow dee! Dray wara yow dee! The eye of the Sun, the eye of the Moon, and my own unrestful eyes—all three are one—all three are one!

There was a city the name whereof I have forgotten, and there the Voice called all night. That was ten days ago. It has cheated me afresh.

I have come hither from a place called Hamirpur, and, behold, it is my Fate that I should meet with thee to my comfort, and the increase of friendship. This is a good omen. By the joy of looking upon thy face the weariness has gone from my feet, and the sorrow of my so long travel is forgotten. Also my heart is peaceful; for I know that the end is near.

It may be that I shall find Daoud Shah in this city going northward, since a Hillman will ever head back to his Hills when the spring warns. And shall he see those hills of our country? Surely I shall overtake him! Surely my vengeance is safe! Surely God hath him in the hollow of His hand against my claiming! There shall no harm befall Daoud Shah till I come; for I would fain kill him quick and whole with the life sticking firm in his body. A pomegranate is sweetest when the cloves break away unwilling from the rind. Let it be in the daytime, that I may see his face, and my delight may be crowned.

And when I have accomplished the matter and my Honour is made clean, I shall return thanks unto God, the Holder of the Scales of the Law, and I shall sleep. From the night, through the day, and into the night again I shall sleep; and no dream shall trouble me.

And now, O my brother, the tale is all told. Ahi! Ahi! Alghias! Ahi!

The Judgment of Dungara

They tell the tale even now among the groves of the Berbulda Hills, and for corroboration point to the roofless and windowless Mission-house. The great God Dungara, the God of Things as They

11

Are, Most Terrible, One-eyed, Bearing the Red Elephant Tusk, did it all; and he who refuses to believe in Dungara will assuredly be smitten by the Madness of Yat—the madness that fell upon the sons and the daughters of the Buria Kol when they turned aside from Dungara and put on clothes. So says Athon Dazé, who is High Priest of the shrine and Warden of the Red Elephant Tusk. But if you ask the Assistant Collector and Agent in Charge of the Buria Kol, he will laugh—not because he bears any malice against missions, but because he himself saw the vengeance of Dungara executed upon the spiritual children of the Reverend Justus Krenk, Pastor of the Tubingen Mission, and upon Lotte, his virtuous wife.

Yet if ever a man merited good treatment of the Gods it was the Reverend Justus, one time of Heidelberg, who, on the faith of a call, went into the wilderness and took the blonde, blue-eyed Lotte with him. 'We will these Heathen now by idolatrous practices so darkened better make,' said Justus in the early days of his career. 'Yes,' he added with conviction, 'they shall good be and shall with their hands to work learn. For all good Christians must work.' And upon a stipend more modest even than that of an English lay-reader, Justus Krenk kept house beyond Kamala and the gorge of Malair, beyond the Berbulda River close to the foot of the blue hill of Panth on whose summit stands the Temple of Dungara—in the heart of the country of the Buria Kol—the naked, good-tempered, timid, shameless, lazy Buria Kol.

Do you know what life at a Mission outpost means? Try to imagine a loneliness exceeding that of the smallest station to which Government has ever sent you—isolation that weighs upon the waking eyelids and drives you by force headlong into the labours of the day. There is no post, there is no one of your own colour to speak to, there are no roads: there is, indeed, food to keep you alive, but it is not pleasant to eat; and whatever of good or beauty or interest there is in your life, must come from yourself and the grace that may be planted in you.

In the morning, with a patter of soft feet, the converts, the doubtful, and the open scoffers troop up to the veranda. You must be infinitely kind and patient, and, above all, clear-sighted, for you deal with the simplicity of childhood, the experience of man, and the subtlety of the savage. Your congregation have a hundred material wants to be considered; and it is for you, as you believe in your personal responsibility to your Maker, to pick out of the clamouring crowd any grain of spirituality that may lie therein. If to the cure of souls you add that of bodies, your task will be all the more difficult, for the sick and the maimed will profess any and every creed for the sake of healing, and will laugh at you because you are simple enough to believe them.

As the day wears and the impetus of the morning dies away, there will come upon you an overwhelming sense of the uselessness of your toil. This must be striven against, and the only spur in your side will be the belief that you are playing against the Devil for the living soul. It is a great, a joyous belief. But he who can hold it unwavering for four-and-twenty consecutive hours must be blessed with an abundantly strong physique and equable nerve.

Ask the grey heads of the Bannockburn Medical Crusade what manner of life their preachers lead; speak to the Racine Gospel Agency, those lean Americans whose boast is that they go where no Englishman dare follow; get a Pastor of the

Tubingen Mission to talk of his experiences—if you can. You will be referred to the printed reports, but these contain no mention of the men who have lost youth and health, all that a man may lose except faith, in the wilds; of English maidens who have gone forth and died in the fever stricken jungle of the Panth Hills, knowing from the first that death was almost a certainty. Few Pastors will tell you of these things any more than they will speak of that young David of St. Bees, who, set apart for the Lord's work, broke down in the utter desolation, and returned half distraught to the Head Mission, crying, 'There is no God, but I have walked with the Devil!'

The reports are silent here, because heroism, failure, doubt, despair, and self-abnegation on the part of a mere cultured white man are things of no weight as compared to the saving of one half-human soul from a fantastic faith in wood-spirits, goblins of the rock, and river-fiends.

And Gallio, the Assistant Collector of the countryside, 'cared for none of these things.' He had been long in the District, and the Buria Kol loved him and brought him offerings of speared fish, orchids from the dim moist heart of the forests, and as much game as he could eat. In return, he gave them quinine, and with Athon Dazé, the High Priest, controlled their simple policies.

'When you have been some years in the country,' said Gallio at the Krenks' table, 'you get to find one creed as good as another. I'll give you all the assistance in my power, of course, but don't hurt my Buria Kol. They are a good people and they trust me.'

'I will them the Word of the Lord teach,' said Justus, his round face beaming with enthusiasm, 'and I will assuredly to their prejudices no wrong hastily without thinking make. But, O my friend, this in the mind impartiality-of-creed-judgment-belooking is very bad.'

'Heigh-ho!' said Gallio. 'I have their bodies and the District to see to, but you can try what you can do for their souls. Only don't behave as your predecessor did, or I'm afraid that I can't guarantee your life.'

'And that?' said Lotte sturdily, handing him a cup of tea.

'He went up to the Temple of Dungara—to be sure, he was new to the country—and began hammering old Dungara over the head with an umbrella; so the Buria Kol turned out and hammered him rather savagely. I was in the District, and he sent a runner to me with a note saying "Persecuted for the Lord's sake. Send wing of regiment." The nearest troops were about two hundred miles off, but I guessed what he had been doing. I rode to Panth and talked to old Athon Dazé like a father, telling him that a man of his wisdom ought to have known that the Sahib had sunstroke and was mad. You never saw a people more sorry in your life. Athon Dazé apologised, sent wood and milk and fowls and all sorts of things; and I gave five rupees to the shrine and told Macnamara that he had been injudicious. He said that I had bowed down in the House of Rimmon; but if he had only just gone over the brow of the hill and insulted Palin Deo, the idol of the Suria Kol, he would have been impaled on a charred bamboo long before I could have done anything, and then I should have had to hang some of the poor brutes. Be gentle with them, Padre—but I don't think you'll do much.'

'Not I,' said Justus, 'but my Master. We will with the little children begin. Many of them will be sick—that is so. After the children the mothers; and then the men. But I would greatly prefer that you in internal sympathies with us were.'

Gallio departed to risk his life in mending the rotten bamboo bridges of his people, in killing a too persistent tiger here or there, in sleeping out in the reeking jungle, or in tracking the Suria Kol raiders who had taken a few heads from their brethren of the Buria clan. He was a knockkneed, shambling young man, naturally devoid of creed or reverence, with a longing for absolute power which his undesirable District gratified.

'No one wants my post,' he used to say grimly, 'and my Collector only pokes his nose in when he's quite certain that there is no fever. I'm monarch of all I survey, and Athon Dazé is my viceroy.'

Because Gallio prided himself on his supreme disregard of human life—though he never extended the theory beyond his own—he naturally rode forty miles to the Mission with a tiny brown girl-baby on his saddle-bow.

'Here is something for you, Padre,' said he. 'The Kols leave their surplus children to die. Don't see why they shouldn't, but you may rear this one. I picked it up beyond the Berbulda forks. I've a notion that the mother has been following me through the woods ever since.'

'It is the first of the fold,' said Justus, and Lotte caught up the screaming morsel to her bosom and hushed it craftily; while, as a wolf hangs in the field, Matui who had borne it, and in accordance with the law of her tribe had exposed it to die, panted weary and footsore in the bamboo-brake, watching the house with hungry mother-eyes. What would the omnipotent Assistant Collector do? Would the little man in the black coat eat her daughter alive, as Athon Dazé said was the custom of all men in black coats?

Matui waited among the bamboos through the long night; and, in the morning, there came forth a fair white woman, the like of whom Matui had never seen, and in her arms was Matui's daughter clad in spotless raiment. Lotte knew little of the tongue of the Buria Kol, but when mother calls to mother, speech is easy to follow. By the hands stretched timidly to the hem of her gown, by the passionate gutturals and the longing eyes, Lotte understood with whom she had to deal. So Matui took her child again—would be a servant, even a slave, to this wonderful white woman, for her own tribe would recognise her no more. And Lotte wept with her exhaustively, after the German fashion, which includes much blowing of the nose.

'First the Child, then the Mother, and last the Man, and to the Glory of God all,' said Justus the Hopeful. And the man came, with a bow and arrows, very angry indeed, for there was no one to cook for him.

But the tale of the Mission is a long one, and I have no space to show how Justus, forgetful of his injudicious predecessor, grievously smote Moto, the husband of Matui, for his brutality; how Moto was startled, but being released from the fear of instant death, took heart and became the faithful ally and first convert of Justus; how the little gathering grew, to the huge disgust of Athon Dazé; how the Priest of the God of Things as They Are argued subtility with the Priest of the God of Things as They Should Be, and was worsted; how the dues of the Temple of Dungara fell away in fowls and fish and honeycomb; how Lotte lightened the Curse of Eve among the women, and how Justus did his best to introduce the Curse of Adam; how the Buria Kol rebelled at this, saying that their God was an idle God, and how Justus partially overcame their scruples against work, and taught them that the black earth was rich in other produce than pig-nuts only.

All these things belong to the history of many months, and throughout those months the white-haired Athon Dazé meditated revenge for the tribal neglect of Dungara. With savage cunning he feigned friendship towards Justus, even hinting at his own conversion; but to the congregation of Dungara he said darkly: 'They of the Padre's flock have put on clothes and worship a busy God. Therefore Dungara will afflict them grievously till they throw themselves, howling, into the waters of the Berbulda.' At night the Red Elephant Tusk boomed and groaned among the hills, and the faithful waked and said: 'The God of Things as They Are matures revenge against the backsliders. Be merciful, Dungara, to us Thy children, and give us all their crops!'

Late in the cold weather the Collector and his wife came into the Buria Kol country. 'Go and look at Krenk's Mission,' said Gallio. 'He is doing good work in his own way, and I think he'd be pleased if you opened the bamboo chapel that he has managed to run up. At any rate you'll see a civilised Buria Kol.'

Great was the stir in the Mission. 'Now he and the gracious lady will that we have done good work with their own eyes see, and—yes— we will him our converts in all their by their own hands constructed new clothes exhibit. It will a great day be—for the Lord always,' said Justus; and Lotte said 'Amen.'

Justus had, in his quiet way, felt jealous of the Basel Weaving Mission, his own converts being unhandy; but Athon Dazé had latterly induced some of them to hackle the glossy silky fibres of a plant that grew plenteously on the Panth Hills. It yielded a cloth white and smooth almost as the tappa of the South Seas, and that day the converts were to wear for the first time clothes made therefrom. Justus was proud of his work.

'They shall in white clothes clothed to meet the Collector and his well-born lady come down, singing "Now thank we all our God." Then he will the Chapel open, and—yes—even Gallio to believe will begin. Stand so, my children, two by two, and—Lotte, why do they thus themselves bescratch? It is not seemly to wriggle, Nala, my child. The Collector will be here and be pained.'

The Collector, his wife, and Gallio climbed the hill to the Mission-station. The converts were drawn up in two lines, a shining band nearly forty strong. 'Hah!' said the Collector, whose acquisitive bent of mind led him to believe that he had fostered the institution from the first. 'Advancing, I see, by leaps and bounds.'

Never was truer word spoken! The Mission was advancing exactly as he had said—at first by little hops and shuffles of shamefaced uneasiness, but soon by the leaps of fly-stung horses and the bounds of maddened kangaroos. From the hill of Panth the Red Elephant Tusk delivered a dry and anguished blare. The ranks of the converts wavered, broke, and scattered with yells and shrieks of pain, while Justus and Lotte stood horror-stricken.

'It is the Judgment of Dungara!' shouted a voice. 'I burn! I burn! To the river or we die!'

The mob wheeled and headed for the rocks that overhung the Berbulda, writhing, stamping, twisting, and shedding its garments as it ran, pursued by the thunder of the trumpet of Dungara. Justus and Lotte fled to the Collector almost in tears.

'I cannot understand! Yesterday,' panted Justus, 'they had the Ten Commandments.—What is this? Praise the Lord, all good spirits by land and by sea! Nala! Oh, shame!'

With a bound and a scream there alighted on the rocks above their heads, Nala, once the pride of the Mission, a maiden of fourteen summers, good, docile, and virtuous—now naked as the dawn and spitting like a wild-cat.

'Was it for this?' she raved, hurling her petticoat at Justus; 'was it for this I left my people and Dungara—for the fires of your Bad Place? Blind ape, little earth-worm, dried fish that you are, you said that I should never burn! O Dungara, I burn now! I burn now! Have mercy, God of Things as They Are! '

She turned and flung herself into the Berbulda, and the trumpet of Dungara bellowed jubilantly. The last of the converts of the Tubingen Mission had put a quarter of a mile of rapid river between herself and her teachers.

'Yesterday,' gulped Justus, 'she taught in the school A, B, C, D.—Oh! It is the work of Satan!'

But Gallio was curiously regarding the maiden's petticoat where it had fallen at his feet. He felt its texture, drew back his shirt-sleeve beyond the deep tan of his wrist and pressed a fold of the cloth against the flesh. A blotch of angry red rose on the white skin.

'Ah!' said Gallio calmly, 'I thought so.'

'What is it?' said Justus.

'I should call it the Shirt of Nessus, but—where did you get the fibre of this cloth from?'

'Athon Dazé,' said Justus. 'He showed the boys how it should manufactured be.'

'The old fox! Do you know that he has given you the Nilgiri Nettle—scorpion—Girardenia heterophylla—to work up. No wonder they squirmed! Why, it stings even when they make bridge-ropes of it unless it's soaked for six weeks. The cunning brute! It would take about half an hour to burn through their thick hides, and then——!'

Gallio burst into laughter, but Lotte was weeping in the arms of the Collector's wife, and Justus had covered his face with his hands.

'Girardenia heterophylla!' repeated Gallio. 'Krenk, why didn't you tell me? I could have saved you this. Woven fire! Anybody but a naked Kol would have known it, and, if I'm a judge of their ways, you'll never get them back.'

He looked across the river to where the converts were still wallowing and wailing in the shallows, and the laughter died out of his eyes, for he saw that the Tubingen Mission to the Buria Kol was dead.

Never again, though they hung mournfully round the deserted school for three months, could Lotte or Justus coax back even the most promising of their flock. No! The end of conversion was the fire of the Bad Place—fire that ran through the limbs and gnawed into the bones. Who dare a second time tempt the anger of Dungara? Let the little man and his wife go elsewhere. The Buria Kol would have none of them. An unofficial message to Athon Dazé that if a hair of their heads were touched, Athon Dazé and the priests of Dungara would be hanged by Gallio at the temple shrine, protected Justus and Lotte from the stumpy poisoned arrows of the Buria Kol, but neither fish nor fowl, honeycomb, salt, nor young pig were brought to their doors any more. And, alas! man cannot live by grace alone if meat be wanting.

'Let us go, mine wife,' said Justus; 'there is no good here, and the Lord has willed that some other man shall the work take—in good time—in His own good time. We will away go, and I will—yes— some botany bestudy.'

If any one is anxious to convert the Buria Kol afresh, there lies at least the core of a Mission-house under the hill of Panth. But the chapel and school have long since fallen back into jungle.

At Howli Thana

AS a messenger, if the heart of the Presence be moved to so great favour. And on six rupees. Yes, Sahib, for I have three little, little children whose stomachs are always empty, and corn is now but forty pounds to the rupee. I will make so clever a messenger that you shall all day long be pleased with me, and, at the end of the year, shall bestow a turban. I know all the roads of the station and many other things. Aha, Sahib! I am clever. Give me service. I was aforetime in the Police. A bad character? Now without doubt an enemy has told this tale. Never was I a scamp. I am a man of clean heart, and all my words are true. They knew this when I was in the Police. They said: 'Afzal Khan is a true speaker in whose words men may trust.' I am a Delhi Pathan, Sahib. All Delhi Pathans are good men. You have seen Delhi? Yes, it is true that there be many scamps among the Delhi Pathans. How wise is the Sahib! Nothing is hid from his eyes, and he will make me his messenger, and I will take all his notes secretly and without ostentation. Nay, Sahib, God is my witness that I meant no evil. I have long desired to serve under a true Sahib—a virtuous Sahib. Many young Sahibs are as devils unchained. With these Sahibs I would take no service—not though all the stomachs of my little children were crying for bread.

Why am I not still in the Police? I will speak true talk. An evil came to the Thana—to Ram Baksh, the Havildar, and Maula Baksh, and Juggut Ram, and Bhim Singh, and Suruj Bul. Ram Baksh is in the jail for a space, and so also is Maula Baksh.

It was at the Thana of Howli, on the road that leads to Gokral-Seetarun wherein are many dacoits. We were all brave men — Rustums. Wherefore we were sent to that Thana, which was eight miles from the next Thana. All day and all night we watched for dacoits. Why does the Sahib laugh? Nay, I will make a confession. The dacoits were too clever, and, seeing this, we made no further trouble. It was in the hot weather. What can a man do in the hot days? Is the Sahib who is so strong—is he, even, vigorous in that hour? We made an arrangement with the dacoits for the sake of peace. That was the work of the Havildar, who was fat. Ho! ho! Sahib, he is now getting thin in the jail among the carpets. The Havildar said: 'Give us no trouble, and we will give you no trouble. At the end of the reaping send us a man to lead before the judge, a man of infirm mind against whom the trumped-up case will break down. Thus we shall save our honour.' To this talk the dacoits agreed, and we had no trouble at the Thana, and could eat melons in peace, sitting upon our charpoys all day long. Sweet as sugar-cane are the melons of Howli!

Now there was an Assistant Commissioner—a Stunt Sahib, in that district, called Yunkum Sahib. Aha! He was hard—hard even as is the Sahib who, without doubt, will give me the shadow of his protection. Many eyes had Yunkum Sahib, and moved quickly through his District. Men called him The Tiger of Gokral-Seetarun, because he would arrive unannounced and make his kill, and, before sunset, would be giving trouble to the Tehsildars thirty miles away. No one knew the comings or the goings of Yunkum Sahib. He had no camp, and when his horse was weary he rode upon a devil-carriage. I do not know its name, but the Sahib sat in the midst of three silver wheels that made no creaking, and drave them with his legs, prancing like a bean-fed horse—thus. A shadow of a hawk upon the fields was not more without noise than the devil-carriage of Yunkum Sahib. It was here: it was there: it was gone: and the rapport was made, and there was trouble. Ask the Tehsildar of Rohestri how the hen-stealings came to be known, Sahib.

It fell upon a night that we of the Thana slept according to custom upon our charpoys, having eaten the evening meal and drunk tobacco. When we awoke in the morning, behold, of our six rifles not one remained! Also, the big Police-book that was in the Havildar's charge was gone. Seeing these things, we were very much afraid, thinking on our parts that the dacoits, regardless of honour, had come by night, and put us to shame. Then said Ram Baksh, the Havildar: 'Be silent! The business is an evil business, but it may yet go well. Let us make the case complete. Bring a kid and my tulwar. See you not now, O fools? A kick for a horse, but for a man a word is enough.'

We of the Thana, perceiving quickly what was in the mind of the Havildar, and greatly fearing that the service would be lost, made haste to take the kid into the inner room, and attended to the words of the Havildar. 'Twenty dacoits came,' said the Havildar, and we, taking his words, repeated after him according to custom. 'There was a great fight,' said the Havildar, 'and of us no man escaped unhurt. The bars of the window were broken. Suruj Bul, see thou to that; and, O men, put speed into your work, for a runner must go with the news to The Tiger of Gokral-Seetarun.' Thereon, Suruj Bul, leaning with his shoulder, brake in the bars of the window, and I, beating her with a whip, made the Havildar's mare skip among the melon-beds till they were much trodden with hoof-prints.

These things being made, I returned to the Thana, and the goat was slain, and certain portions of the walls were blackened with fire, and each man dipped his clothes a little into the blood of the goat. Know, O Sahib, that a wound made by man upon his own body can, by those skilled, be easily discerned from a wound wrought by another man. Therefore, the Havildar, taking his tulwar, smote one of us lightly on the forearm in the fat, and another on the leg, and a third on the back of the hand. Thus dealt he with all of us till the blood came; and Suruj Bul, more eager than the others, took out much hair. O Sahib, never was so perfect an arrangement. Yea, even I would have sworn that the Thana had been treated as we said. There was smoke and breaking and blood and trampled earth.

'Ride now, Maula Baksh,' said the Havildar, 'to the house of the Stunt Sahib, and carry the news of the dacoity. Do you also, O Afzal Khan, run there, and take heed that you are mired with sweat and dust on your incoming. The blood will be dry on the clothes. I will stay and send a straight rapport to the Dipty Sahib, and we will catch certain that ye know of, villagers, so that all may be ready against the Dipty Sahib's arrival.'

Thus Maula Baksh rode, and I ran hanging on the stirrup, and together we came in an evil plight before The Tiger of Gokral-Seetarun in the Rohestri tehsil. Our tale was long and correct, Sahib, for we gave even the names of the dacoits and the issue of the fight, and besought him to come. But The Tiger made no sign, and only smiled after the manner of Sahibs when they have a wickedness in their hearts. 'Swear ye to the rapport?' said he, and we said: 'Thy servants swear. The blood of the fight is but newly dry upon us. Judge thou if it be the blood of the servants of the Presence, or not.' And he said 'I see. Ye have done well.' But he did not call for his horse or his devil-carriage, and scour the land as was his custom. He said: 'Rest now and eat bread, for ye be wearied men. I will wait the coming of the Dipty Sahib.'

Now it is the order that the Havildar of the Thana should send a straight rapport of all dacoities to the Dipty Sahib. At noon came he, a fat man and an old, and overbearing withal, but we of the Thana had no fear of his anger, dreading more the silences of The Tiger of Gokral-Seetarun. With him came Ram Baksh, the Havildar, and the others, guarding ten men of the village of Howli—all men evil affected towards the Police of the Sirkar. As prisoners they came, the irons upon their hands, crying for mercy—Imam Baksh, the farmer, who had denied his wife to the Havildar, and others, ill-conditioned rascals against whom we of the Thana bore spite. It was well done, and the Havildar was proud. But the Dipty Sahib was angry with the Stunt Sahib for lack of zeal, and said 'Dam-Dam' after the custom of the English people, and extolled the Havildar. Yunkum Sahib lay still in his long chair. 'Have the men sworn?' said Yunkum Sahib. 'Ay, and captured ten evildoers,' said the Dipty Sahib. 'There be more abroad in your charge. Take horse-ride, and go in the name of the Sirkar!' 'Truly there be more evildoers abroad,' said Yunkum Sahib, 'but there is no need of a horse. Come all men with me.'

I saw the mark of a string on the temples of Imam Baksh. Does the Presence know the torture of the Cold Draw? I saw also the face of The Tiger of Gokral-Seetarun, the evil smile was upon it, and I stood back ready for what might befall. Well it was, Sahib, that I did this thing. Yunkum Sahib unlocked the door of his bathroom, and smiled anew. Within lay the six rifles and the big Police-book of the Thana of Howli! He had come by night in the devil-carriage that is noiseless as a ghoul, and, moving among us asleep, had taken away both the guns and the book! Twice had he come to the Thana, taking each time three rifles. The liver of the Havildar was turned to water, and he fell scrabbling in the dirt about the boots of Yunkum Sahib, crying 'Have mercy! '

And I? Sahib, I am a Delhi Pathan, and a young man with little children. The Havildar's mare was in the compound. I ran to her and rode. The black wrath of the Sirkar was behind me, and I knew not whither to go. Till she dropped and died I rode the red mare; and by the blessing of God, Who is without doubt on the side of all just men, I escaped. But the Havildar and the rest are now in jail.

I am a scamp? It is as the Presence pleases. God will make the Presence a Lord, and give him a rich Memsahib as fair as a Peri to wife, and many strong sons, if he makes me his orderly. The Mercy of Heaven be upon the Sahib! Yes, I will only go to the Bazar and bring my children to these so-palace-like quarters, and then—the Presence is my Father and my Mother, and I, Afzal Khan, am his slave.

Ohé, Sirdar-ji! I also am of the household of the Sahib.

At Howli Thana

AS a messenger, if the heart of the Presence be moved to so great favour. And on six rupees. Yes, Sahib, for I have three little, little children whose stomachs are always empty, and corn is now but forty pounds to the rupee. I will make so clever a messenger that you shall all day long be pleased with me, and, at the end of the year, shall bestow a turban. I know all the roads of the station and many other things. Aha, Sahib! I am clever. Give me service. I was aforetime in the Police. A bad character? Now without doubt an enemy has told this tale. Never was I a scamp. I am a man of clean heart, and all my words are true. They knew this when I was in the Police. They said: 'Afzal Khan is a true speaker in whose words men may trust.' I am a Delhi Pathan, Sahib. All Delhi Pathans are good men. You have seen Delhi? Yes, it is true that there be many scamps among the Delhi Pathans. How wise is the Sahib! Nothing is hid from his eyes, and he will make me his messenger, and I will take all his notes secretly and without ostentation. Nay, Sahib, God is my witness that I meant no evil. I have long desired to serve under a true Sahib—a virtuous Sahib. Many young Sahibs are as devils unchained. With these Sahibs I would take no service—not though all the stomachs of my little children were crying for bread.

Why am I not still in the Police? I will speak true talk. An evil came to the Thana—to Ram Baksh, the Havildar, and Maula Baksh, and Juggut Ram, and Bhim Singh, and Suruj Bul. Ram Baksh is in the jail for a space, and so also is Maula Baksh.

It was at the Thana of Howli, on the road that leads to Gokral-Seetarun wherein are many dacoits. We were all brave men—Rustums. Wherefore we were sent to that Thana, which was eight miles from the next Thana. All day and all night we watched for dacoits. Why does the Sahib laugh? Nay, I will make a confession. The dacoits were too clever, and, seeing this, we made no further trouble. It was in the hot weather. What can a man do in the hot days? Is the Sahib who is so strong—is he, even, vigorous in that hour? We made an arrangement with the dacoits for the sake of peace. That was the work of the Havildar, who was fat. Ho! ho! Sahib, he is now getting thin in the jail among the carpets. The Havildar said: 'Give us no trouble, and we will give you no trouble. At the end of the reaping send us a man to lead before the judge, a man of infirm mind against whom the trumped-up case will break down. Thus we shall save our honour.' To this talk the dacoits agreed, and we had no trouble at the Thana, and could eat melons in peace, sitting upon our charpoys all day long. Sweet as sugar-cane are the melons of Howli!

Now there was an Assistant Commissioner—a Stunt Sahib, in that district, called Yunkum Sahib. Aha! He was hard—hard even as is the Sahib who, without doubt, will give me the shadow of his protection. Many eyes had Yunkum Sahib, and moved quickly through his District. Men called him The Tiger of Gokral-Seetarun, because he would arrive unannounced and make his kill, and, before sunset, would be giving trouble to the Tehsildars thirty miles away. No one knew the comings or the goings of Yunkum Sahib. He had no camp, and when his horse was weary he rode upon a devil-carriage. I do not know its name, but the Sahib sat in the midst of three silver wheels that made no creaking, and drave them with his legs, prancing like a bean-fed horse—thus. A shadow of a hawk upon the fields was not more without noise than the devil-carriage of Yunkum Sahib. It was here: it was there: it was gone: and the rapport was made, and there was trouble. Ask the Tehsildar of Rohestri how the hen-stealings came to be known, Sahib.

It fell upon a night that we of the Thana slept according to custom upon our charpoys, having eaten the evening meal and drunk tobacco. When we awoke in the morning, behold, of our six rifles not one remained! Also, the big Police-book that was in the Havildar's charge was gone. Seeing these things, we were very much afraid, thinking on our parts that the dacoits, regardless of honour, had come by night, and put us to shame. Then said Ram Baksh, the Havildar: 'Be silent! The business is an evil business, but it may yet go well. Let us make the case complete. Bring a kid and my tulwar. See you not now, O fools? A kick for a horse, but for a man a word is enough.'

We of the Thana, perceiving quickly what was in the mind of the Havildar, and greatly fearing that the service would be lost, made haste to take the kid into the inner room, and attended to the words of the Havildar. 'Twenty dacoits came,' said the Havildar, and we, taking his words, repeated after him according to custom. 'There was a great fight,' said the Havildar, 'and of us no man escaped unhurt. The bars of the window were broken. Suruj Bul, see thou to that; and, O men, put speed into your work, for a runner must go with the news to The Tiger of Gokral-Seetarun.' Thereon, Suruj Bul, leaning with his shoulder, brake in the bars of the window, and I, beating her with a whip, made the Havildar's mare skip among the melon-beds till they were much trodden with hoof-prints.

These things being made, I returned to the Thana, and the goat was slain, and certain portions of the walls were blackened with fire, and each man dipped his clothes a little into the blood of the goat. Know, O Sahib, that a wound made by man upon his own body can, by those skilled, be easily discerned from a wound wrought by another man. Therefore, the Havildar, taking his tulwar, smote one of us lightly on the forearm in the fat, and another on the leg, and a third on the back of the hand. Thus dealt he with all of us till the blood came; and Suruj Bul, more eager than the others, took out much hair. O Sahib, never was so perfect an arrangement. Yea, even I would have sworn that the Thana had been treated as we said. There was smoke and breaking and blood and trampled earth.

'Ride now, Maula Baksh,' said the Havildar, 'to the house of the Stunt Sahib, and carry the news of the dacoity. Do you also, O Afzal Khan, run there, and take heed that you are mired with sweat and dust on your incoming. The blood will be dry on the clothes. I will stay and send a straight rapport to the Dipty Sahib, and we will catch certain that ye know of, villagers, so that all may be ready against the Dipty Sahib's arrival.'

Thus Maula Baksh rode, and I ran hanging on the stirrup, and together we came in an evil plight before The Tiger of Gokral-Seetarun in the Rohestri tehsil. Our tale was long and correct, Sahib, for we gave even the names of the dacoits and the issue of the fight, and besought him to come. But The Tiger made no sign, and only smiled after the manner of Sahibs when they have a wickedness in their hearts. 'Swear ye to the rapport?' said he, and we said: 'Thy servants swear. The blood of the fight is but newly dry upon us. Judge thou if it be the blood of the servants of the Presence, or not.' And he said 'I see. Ye have done well.' But he did not call for his horse or his devil-carriage, and scour the land as was his custom. He said: 'Rest now and eat bread, for ye be wearied men. I will wait the coming of the Dipty Sahib.'

Now it is the order that the Havildar of the Thana should send a straight rapport of all dacoities to the Dipty Sahib. At noon came he, a fat man and an old, and overbearing withal, but we of the Thana had no fear of his anger, dreading more the silences of The Tiger of Gokral-Seetarun. With him came Ram Baksh, the Havildar, and the others, guarding ten men of the village of Howli—all men evil affected towards the Police of the Sirkar. As prisoners they came, the irons upon their hands, crying for mercy—Imam Baksh, the farmer, who had denied his wife to the Havildar, and others, ill-conditioned rascals against whom we of the Thana bore spite. It was well done, and the Havildar was proud. But the Dipty Sahib was angry with the Stunt Sahib for lack of zeal, and said 'Dam-Dam' after the custom of the English people, and extolled the Havildar. Yunkum Sahib lay still in his long chair. 'Have the men sworn?' said Yunkum Sahib. 'Ay, and captured ten evildoers,' said the Dipty Sahib. 'There be more abroad in your charge. Take horse-ride, and go in the name of the Sirkar!' 'Truly there be more evildoers abroad,' said Yunkum Sahib, 'but there is no need of a horse. Come all men with me.'

I saw the mark of a string on the temples of Imam Baksh. Does the Presence know the torture of the Cold Draw? I saw also the face of The Tiger of Gokral-Seetarun, the evil smile was upon it, and I stood back ready for what might befall. Well it was, Sahib, that I did this thing. Yunkum Sahib unlocked the door of his bathroom, and smiled anew. Within lay the six rifles and the big Police-book of the Thana of Howli! He had come by night in the devil-carriage that is noiseless as a ghoul, and, moving among us asleep, had taken away both the guns and the book! Twice had he come to the Thana, taking each time three rifles. The liver of the Havildar was turned to water, and he fell scrabbling in the dirt about the boots of Yunkum Sahib, crying 'Have mercy! '

And I? Sahib, I am a Delhi Pathan, and a young man with little children. The Havildar's mare was in the compound. I ran to her and rode. The black wrath of the Sirkar was behind me, and I knew not whither to go. Till she dropped and died I rode the red mare; and by the blessing of God, Who is without doubt on the side of all just men, I escaped. But the Havildar and the rest are now in jail.

I am a scamp? It is as the Presence pleases. God will make the Presence a Lord, and give him a rich Memsahib as fair as a Peri to wife, and many strong sons, if he makes me his orderly. The Mercy of Heaven be upon the Sahib! Yes, I will only go to the Bazar and bring my children to these so-palace-like quarters, and then—the Presence is my Father and my Mother, and I, Afzal Khan, am his slave.

Ohé, Sirdar-ji! I also am of the household of the Sahib.

Gemini

This is your English Justice, Protector of the Poor. Look at my back and loins which are beaten with sticks—heavy sticks! I am a poor man, and there is no justice in Courts.

There were two of us, and we were born of one birth, but I swear to you that I was born the first, and Ram Dass is the younger by three full breaths. The astrologer said so, and it is written in my horoscope—the horoscope of Durga Dass.

But we were alike—I and my brother, who is a beast without honour—so alike that none knew, together or apart, which was Durga Dass. I am a Mahajun of Pali in Marwar, and an honest man. This is true talk. When we were men, we left our father's house in Pali, and went to the Punjab, where all the people are mud-heads and sons of asses. We took shop together in Isser Jang—I and my brother—near the big well where the Governor's camp draws water. But Ram Dass, who is without truth, made quarrel with me, and we were divided. He took his books, and his pots, and his Mark, and became a bunnia—a money-lender—in the long street of Isser Jang, near the gateway of the road that goes to Montgomery. It was not my fault that we pulled each other's turban. I am a Mahajun of Pali, and I always speak true talk. Ram Dass was the thief and the liar.

Now no man, not even the little children, could at one glance see which was Ram Dass and which was Durga Dass. But all the people of Isser Jang—may they die without sons!—said that we were thieves. They used much bad talk, but I took money on their bedsteads and their cooking-pots, and the standing crop and the calf unborn, from the well in the big square to the gate of the Montgomery road. They were fools, these people—unfit to cut the toe-nails of a Marwari from Pali. I lent money to them all. A little, very little only—here a pice and there a pice. God is my witness that I am a poor man! The money is all with Ram Dass—may his sons turn Christian, and his daughter be a burning fire and a shame in the house from generation to generation! May she die unwed, and be the mother of a multitude of bastards! Let the light go out in the house of Ram Dass, my brother. This I pray daily twice—with offerings and charms.

Thus the trouble began. We divided the town of Isser Jang between us—I and my brother. There was a landholder beyond the gates, living but one short mile out, on the road that leads to Montgomery, and his name was Mohammed Shah, son of a Nawab. He was a great devil and drank wine. So long as there were women in his house, and wine and money for the marriage-feasts, he was merry and wiped his mouth. Ram Dass lent him the money, a lakh or half a lakh—how do I know?—and so long as the money was lent, the landholder cared not what he signed.

The people of Isser Jang were my portion, and the landholder and the out-town were the portion of Ram Dass; for so we had arranged. I was the poor man, for the people of Isser Jang were without wealth. I did what I could, but Ram Dass had only to wait without the door of the landholder's garden-court, and to lend him the money, taking the bonds from the hand of the steward.

In the autumn of the year after the lending, Ram Dass said to the landholder: 'Pay me my money,' but the landholder gave him abuse. But Ram Dass went into the Courts with the papers and the bonds—all correct—and took out decrees against the landholder; and the name of the Government was across the stamps of the decrees. Ram Dass took field by field, and mango-tree by mango-tree, and well by well; putting in his own men—debtors of the out-town of Isser Jang—to cultivate the crops. So he crept up across the land, for he had the papers, and the name of the Government was across the stamps, till his men held the crops for him on all sides of the big white house of the landholder. It was well done; but when the landholder saw these things he was very angry and cursed Ram Dass after the manner of the Mohammedans.

And thus the landholder was angry, but Ram Dass laughed and claimed more fields, as was written upon the bonds. This was in the month of Phagun. I took my horse and went out to speak to the man who makes lac-bangles upon the road that leads to Montgomery, because he owed me a debt. There was in front of me, upon his horse, my brother Ram Dass. And when he saw me he turned aside into the high crops, because there was hatred between us. And I went forward till I came to the orange-bushes by the landholder's house. The bats were flying, and the evening smoke was low down upon the land. Here met me four men—swashbucklers and Mohammedans—with their faces bound up, laying hold of my horse's bridle and crying out: 'This is Ram Dass! Beat!' Me they beat with their staves—heavy staves bound about with wire at the end, such weapons as those swine of Punjabis use—till, having cried for mercy, I fell down senseless. But these shameless ones still beat me, saying: 'O Ram Dass, this is your interest—well-weighed and counted into your hand, Ram Dass.' I cried aloud that I was not Ram Dass, but Durga Dass, his brother, yet they only beat me the more, and when I could make no more outcry they left me. But I saw their faces. There was Elahi Baksh who runs by the side of the landholder's white horse, and Nur Ali the keeper of the door, and Wajib Ali the very strong cook, and Abdul Latif the messenger—all of the household of the landholder. These things I can swear on the Cow's Tail if need be, but—Ahi!

Ahi!—they have been already sworn, and I am a poor man whose honour is lost.

When these four had gone away laughing, my brother Ram Dass came out of the crops and mourned over me as one dead. But I opened my eyes, and prayed him to get me water. When I had drunk, he carried me on his back, and by byways brought me into the town of Isser Jang. My heart was turned to Ram Dass, my brother, in that hour because of his kindness, and I lost my enmity.

But a snake is a snake till it is dead; and a liar is a liar till the judgment of the Gods takes hold of his heel. I was wrong in that I trusted my brother—the son of my mother.

When we had come to his house and I was a little restored, I told him my tale, and he said 'Without doubt, it is me whom they would have beaten. But the Law Courts are open, and there is the justice of the Sirkar above all; and to the Law Courts do thou go when this sickness is overpast.'

Now when we two had left Pali in the old years, there fell a famine that ran from Jeysulmir to Gurgaon and touched Gogunda in the south. At that time the sister of my father came away and lived with us in Isser Jang; for a man must above all see that his folk do not die of want. When the quarrel between us twain came about, the sister of my father—a lean she-dog without teeth—said that Ram Dass had the right, and went with him. Into her hands—because she knew medicines and many cures—Ram Dass, my brother, put me faint with the beating, and much bruised even to the pouring of blood from the mouth. When I had two days' sickness the fever came upon me; and I set aside the fever to the account written in my mind against the landholder.

The Punjabis of Isser Jang are all the sons of Belial and a she-ass, but they are very good witnesses, bearing testimony unshakenly whatever the pleaders may say. I would purchase witnesses by the score, and each man should give evidence, not only against Nur Ali, Wajib Ali, Abdul Latif, and Elahi Baksh, but against the landholder, saying that he upon his white horse had called his men to beat me; and, further, that they had robbed me of two hundred rupees. For the latter testimony, I would remit a little of the debt of the man who sold the lac-bangles, and he should say that he had put the money into my hands, and had seen the robbery from afar, but, being afraid, had run away. This plan I told to my brother Ram Dass; and he said that the arrangement was good, and bade me take comfort and make swift work to be abroad again. My heart was opened to my brother in my sickness, and I told him the names of those whom I would call as witnesses—all men in my debt, but of that the Magistrate Sahib could have no knowledge, nor the landholder. The fever stayed with me, and after the fever I was taken with colic and gripings very terrible. In that day I thought that my end was at hand, but I know now that she who gave me the medicines, the sister of my father—a widow with a widow's heart— had brought about my second sickness. Ram Dass, my brother, said that my house was shut and locked, and brought me the big door- key and my books, together with all the moneys that were in my house—even the money that was buried under the floor; for I was in great fear lest thieves should break in and dig. I speak true talk; there was but very little money in my house. Perhaps ten rupees— perhaps twenty. How can I tell? God is my witness that I am a poor man.

One night, when I had told Ram Dass all that was in my heart of the lawsuit that I would bring against the landholder, and Ram Dass had said that he had made the arrangements with the witnesses, giving me their names written, I was taken with a new great sickness, and they put me on the bed. When I was a little recovered—I cannot tell how many days afterwards—I made inquiry for Ram Dass, and the sister of my father said that he had gone to Montgomery upon a lawsuit. I took medicine and slept very heavily without waking. When my eyes were opened there was a great stillness in the house of Ram Dass, and none answered when I called—not even the sister of my father. This filled me with fear, for I knew not what had happened.

Taking a stick in my hand, I went out slowly, till I came to the great square by the well, and my heart was hot in me against the landholder because of the pain of every step I took.

I called for Jowar Singh, the carpenter, whose name was first upon the list of those who should bear evidence against the landholder, saying: 'Are all things ready, and do you know what should be said?'

Jowar Singh answered: 'What is this, and whence do you come, Durga Dass?'

I said: 'From my bed, where I have so long lain sick because of the landholder. Where is Ram Dass, my brother, who was to have made the arrangement for the witnesses? Surely you and yours know these things!'

Then Jowar Singh said: 'What has this to do with us, O Liar? I have borne witness and I have been paid, and the landholder has, by the order of the Court, paid both the five hundred rupees that he robbed from Ram Dass and yet other five hundred because of the great injury he did to your brother.'

The well and the jujube-tree above it and the square of Isser Jang became dark in my eyes, but I leaned on my stick and said: 'Nay! This is child's talk and senseless. It was I who suffered at the hands of the landholder, and I am come to make ready the case. Where is my brother Ram Dass?'

But Jowar Singh shook his head, and a woman cried: 'What lie is here? What quarrel had the landholder with you, bunnia? It is only a shameless one and one without faith who profits by his brother's smarts. Have these bunnias no bowels?'

I cried again, saying: 'By the Cow—by the Oath of the Cow, by the Temple of the Blue-throated Mahadeo, I and I only was beaten— beaten to the death! Let your talk be straight, O people of Isser Jang, and I will pay for the witnesses.' And I tottered where I stood, for the sickness and the pain of the beating were heavy upon me.

Then Ram Narain, who has his carpet spread under the jujube-tree by the well, and writes all letters for the men of the town, came up and said: 'To-day is the one-and-fortieth day since the beating, and since these six days the case has been judged in the Court, and the Assistant Commissioner Sahib has given it for your brother Ram Dass, allowing the robbery, to which, too, I bore witness, and all things else as the witnesses said. There were many witnesses, and twice Ram Dass became senseless in the Court because of his wounds, and the Stunt Sahib—the baba Stunt Sahib—gave him a chair before all the pleaders. Why do you howl, Durga Dass? These things fell as I have said. Was it not so?'

And Jowar Singh said: 'That is truth. I was there, and there was a red cushion in the chair.'

And Ram Narain said: 'Great shame has come upon the landholder because of this judgment, and, fearing his anger, Ram Dass and all his house have gone back to Pali. Ram Dass told us that you also had gone first, the enmity being healed between you, to open a shop in Pali. Indeed, it were well for you that you go even now, for the landholder has sworn that if he catch any one of your house, he will hang him by the heels from the well-beam, and, swinging him to and fro, will beat him with staves till the blood runs from his ears. What I have said in respect to the case is true, as these men here can testify—even to the five hundred rupees.'

I said: 'Was it five hundred?' And Kirpa Ram, the Jat, said: 'Five hundred; for I bore witness also.'

And I groaned, for it had been in my heart to have said two hundred only.

Then a new fear came upon me and my bowels turned to water, and, running swiftly to the house of Ram Dass, I sought for my books and my money in the great wooden chest under my bedstead. There remained nothing—not even a cowrie's value. All had been taken by the devil who said he was my brother. I went to my own house also and opened the boards of the shutters; but there also was nothing save the rats among the grain-baskets. In that hour my senses left me, and, tearing my clothes, I ran to the well-place, crying out for the justice of the English on my brother Ram Dass, and, in my madness, telling all that the books were lost. When men saw that I would have jumped down the well they believed the truth of my talk, more especially because upon my back and bosom were still the marks of the staves of the landholder.

Jowar Singh the carpenter withstood me, and turning me in his hands—for he is a very strong man—showed the scars upon my body, and bowed down with laughter upon the well-curb. He cried aloud so that all heard him, from the well-square to the Caravanserai of the Pilgrims 'Oho! The jackals have quarrelled, and the grey one has been caught in the trap. In truth, this man has been grievously beaten, and his brother has taken the money which the Court decreed! Oh, bunnia, this shall be told for years against you! The jackals have quarrelled, and, moreover, the books are burned. O people indebted to Durga Dass—and I know that ye be many—the books are burned!'

Then all Isser Jang took up the cry that the books were burned— Ahi! Ahi! that in my folly I had let that escape my mouth—and they laughed throughout the city. They gave me the abuse of the Punjabi, which is a terrible abuse and very hot; pelting me also with sticks and cow-dung till I fell down and cried for mercy.

Ram Narain, the letter-writer, bade the people cease, for fear that the news should get into Montgomery, and the Policemen might come down to inquire. He said, using many bad words 'This much mercy will I do to you, Durga Dass, though there was no mercy in your dealings with my sister's son over the matter of the dun heifer. Has any man a pony on which he sets no store, that this fellow may escape? If the landholder hears that one of the twain (and God knows whether he beat one or both, but this man is certainly beaten) be in the city, there will be a murder done, and then will come the Police, making inquisition into each man's house and eating the sweet-seller's stuff all day long.'

Kirpa Ram, the Jat, said: 'I have a pony very sick. But with beating he can be made to walk for two miles. If he dies, the hide-sellers will have the body.'

Then Chumbo, the hide-seller, said: 'I will pay three annas for the body, and will walk by this man's side till such time as the pony dies. If it be more than two miles, I will pay two annas only.'

Kirpa Ram said: 'Be it so.' Men brought out the pony, and I asked leave to draw a little water from the well, because I was dried up with fear.

Then Ram Narain said: 'Here be four annas. God has brought you very low, Durga Dass, and I would not send you away empty, even though the matter of my sister's son's dun heifer be an open sore between us. It is a long way to your own country. Go, and if it be so willed, live; but, above all, do not take the pony's bridle, for that is mine.'

And I went out of Isser Jang amid the laughing of the huge-thighed Jats, and the hide-seller walked by my side waiting for the pony to fall dead. In one mile it died, and being full of fear of the landholder, I ran till I could run no more, and came to this place.

But I swear by the Cow, I swear by all things whereon Hindus and Mohammedans, and even the Sahibs swear, that I, and not my brother, was beaten by the landholder. But the case is shut, and the doors of the Law Courts are shut, and God knows where the baba Stunt Sahib—the mother's milk is not dry upon his hairless lip—is gone. Ahi! Ahi! I have no witnesses, and the scars will heal, and I am a poor man. But, on my Father's Soul, on the oath of a Mahajun from Pali, I, and not my brother, I was beaten by the landholder!

What can I do? The Justice of the English is as a great river. Having gone forward, it does not return. Howbeit, do you, Sahib, take a pen and write clearly what I have said, that the Dipty Sahib may see, and reprove the Stunt Sahib, who is a colt yet unlicked by the mare, so young is he. I, and not my brother, was beaten, and he is gone to the west—I do not know where.

But, above all things, write—so that the Sahibs may read, and his disgrace be accomplished—that Ram Dass, my brother, son of Purun Dass, Mahajun of Pali, is a swine and a night-thief, a taker of life, an eater of flesh, a jackal-spawn without beauty, or faith, or cleanliness, or honour!

At Twenty-Two

'A weaver went out to reap but stayed to unravel the corn-stalks. Ha! ha! ha! Is there any sense in a weaver?'
Janki Meah glared at Kundoo, but, as Janki Meah was blind, Kundoo was not impressed. He had come to argue with Janki Meah, and, if chance favoured, to make love to the old man's pretty young wife.

This was Kundoo's grievance, and he spoke in the name of all the five men who, with Janki Meah, composed the gang in Number Seven gallery of Twenty-Two. Janki Meah had been blind for the thirty years during which he had served the Jimahari Colliery with pick and crowbar. All through those thirty years he had regularly, every morning before going down, drawn from the overseer his allowance of lamp-oil—just as if he had been an eyed miner. What Kundoo's gang resented, as hundreds of gangs had resented before, was Janki Meah's selfishness.

He would not add the oil to the common stock of his gang, but would save and sell it.

'I knew these workings before you were born,' Janki Meah used to reply. 'I don't want the light to get my coal out by, and I am not going to help you. The oil is mine, and I intend to keep it.'

A strange man in many ways was Janki Meah, the white-haired, hot-tempered, sightless weaver who had turned pitman. All day long— except on Sundays and Mondays when he was usually drunk—he worked in the Twenty-Two shaft of the Jimahari Colliery as cleverly as a man with all the senses. At evening he went up in the great steam-hauled cage to the pit-bank, and there called for his pony—a rusty, coal-dusty beast, nearly as old as Janki Meah. The pony would come to his side, and Janki Meah would clamber on to its back and be taken at once to the plot of land which he, like the other miners, received from the Jimahari Company. The pony knew that place, and when, after six years, the Company changed all the allotments to prevent the miners from acquiring proprietary rights, Janki Meah represented, with tears in his eyes, that were his holding shifted he would never be able to find his way to the new one. 'My horse only knows that place,' pleaded Janki Meah, and so he was allowed to keep his land.

On the strength of this concession and his accumulated oil-savings, Janki Meah took a second wife—a girl of the Jolaha main stock of the Meahs, and singularly beautiful. Janki Meah could not see her beauty; wherefore he took her on trust, and forbade her to go down the pit. He had not worked for thirty years in the dark without knowing that the pit was no place for pretty women. He loaded her with ornaments—not brass or pewter, but real silver ones—and she rewarded him by flirting outrageously with Kundoo of Number Seven gallery gang. Kundoo was really the head of the gang, but Janki Meah insisted upon all the work being entered in his own name, and chose the men that he worked with. Custom—stronger even than the Jimahari Company—dictated that Janki, by right of his years, should manage these things, and should, also, work despite his blindness. In Indian mines, where they cut into the solid coal with the pick and clear it out from floor to ceiling, he could come to no great harm. At Home, where they undercut the coal and bring it down in crashing avalanches from the roof, he would never have been allowed to set foot in a pit. He was not a popular man because of his oil-savings; but all the gangs admitted that Janki knew all the khads, or workings, that had ever been sunk or worked since the Jimahari Company first started operations on the Tarachunda fields.

Pretty little Unda only knew that her old husband was a fool who could be managed. She took no interest in the colliery except in so far as it swallowed up Kundoo five days out of the seven, and covered him with coal-dust. Kundoo was a great workman, and did his best not to get drunk, because, when he had saved forty rupees, Unda was to steal everything that she could find in Janki's house and run with Kundoo to a land where there were no mines, and every one kept three fat bullocks and a milch-buffalo. While this scheme ripened it was his custom to drop in upon Janki and worry him about the oil-savings. Unda sat in a corner and nodded approval. On the night when Kundoo had quoted that objectionable proverb about weavers, Janki grew angry.

'Listen, you pig,' said he. 'Blind I am, and old I am, but, before ever you were born, I was grey among the coal. Even in the days when the Twenty-Two khad was unsunk, and there were not two thousand men here, I was known to have all knowledge of the pits. What khad is there that I do not know, from the bottom of the shaft to the end of the last drive? Is it the Baromba khad, the oldest, or the Twenty-Twos where Tibu's gallery runs up to Number Five?

'Hear the old fool talk!' said Kundoo, nodding to Unda. 'No gallery of Twenty-Two will cut into Five before the end of the Rains. We have a month's solid coal before us. The Babuji says so.'

'Babuji! Pigji! Dogji! What do these fat slugs from Calcutta know? He draws and draws and draws, and talks and talks and talks, and his maps are all wrong. I, Janki, know that this is so. When a man has been shut up in the dark for thirty years God gives him knowledge. The old gallery that Tibu's gang made is not six feet from Number Five.'

'Without doubt God gives the blind knowledge,' said Kundoo, with a look at Unda. 'Let it be as you say. I, for my part, do not know where lies the gallery of Tibu's gang, but I am not a withered monkey who needs oil to grease his joints with.'

Kundoo swung out of the hut laughing, and Unda giggled. Janki turned his sightless eyes towards his wife and swore. 'I have land, and I have sold a great deal of lamp-oil,' mused Janki, 'but I was a fool to marry this child.'

A week later the Rains set in with a vengeance, and the gangs paddled about in coal-slush at the pit-banks. Then the big mine-pumps were made ready, and the Manager of the Colliery ploughed through the wet towards the Tarachunda River swelling between its soppy banks. 'Lord send that this beastly beck doesn't misbehave,' said the Manager piously, and he went to take counsel with his Assistant about the pumps.

But the Tarachunda misbehaved very much indeed. After a fall of three inches of rain in an hour it was obliged to do something. It topped its bank and joined the flood-water that was hemmed between two low hills just where the embankment of the Colliery

43

main line crossed. When a large part of a rain-fed river, and a few acres of flood-water, make a dead set for a nine foot culvert, the culvert may spout its finest, but the water cannot all get out. The Manager pranced upon one leg with excitement, and his language was improper.

He had reason to swear, because he knew that one inch of water on land meant a pressure of one hundred tons to the acre; and here was about five feet of water forming, behind the railway embankment, over the shallower workings of Twenty-Two. You must understand that, in a coal-mine, the coal nearest the surface is worked first from the central shaft. That is to say, the miners may clear out the stuff to within ten, twenty, or thirty feet of the surface, and, when all is worked out, leave only a skin of earth upheld by some few pillars of coal. In a deep mine, where they know that they have any amount of material at hand, men prefer to get all their mineral out at one shaft, rather than make a number of little holes to tap the comparatively unimportant surface-coal.

And the Manager watched the flood.

The culvert spouted a nine-foot gush; but the water still formed, and word was sent to clear the men out of Twenty-Two. The cages came up crammed and crammed again with the men nearest the pit's-eye, as they call the place where you can see daylight from the bottom of the main shaft. All away and away up the long black galleries the flare-lamps were winking and dancing like so many fireflies, and the men and the women waited for the clanking, rattling, thundering cages to come down and fly up again. But the out-workings were very far off, and word could not be passed quickly, though the heads of the gangs and the Assistant shouted and swore and tramped and stumbled. The Manager kept one eye on the great troubled pool behind the embankment, and prayed that the culvert would give way and let the water through in time. With the other eye he watched the cages come up and saw the headman counting the roll of the gangs. With all his heart and soul he swore at the winder who controlled the iron drum that wound up the wire rope on which hung the cages.

In a little time there was a down-draw in the water behind the embankment—a sucking whirlpool, all yellow and yeasty. The water had smashed through the skin of the earth and was pouring into the old shallow workings of Twenty-Two.

Deep down below, a rush of black water caught the last gang waiting for the cage, and as they clambered in, the whirl was about their waists. The cage reached the pit-bank, and the Manager called the roll. The gangs were all safe except Gang Janki, Gang Mogul, and Gang Rahim, eighteen men, with perhaps ten basket-women who loaded the coal into the little iron carriages that ran on the tramways of the main galleries. These gangs were in the out-workings, threequarters of a mile away, on the extreme fringe of the mine. Once more the cage went down, but with only two Englishmen in it, and dropped into a swirling, roaring current that had almost touched the roof of some of the lower side-galleries. One of the wooden balks with which they had propped the old workings shot past on the current, just missing the cage.

'If we don't want our ribs knocked out, we'd better go,' said the Manager. 'We can't even save the Company's props.'

The cage drew out of the water with a splash, and a few minutes later it was officially reported that there was at least ten feet of water in the pit's eye. Now ten feet of water there meant that all other places in the mine were flooded except such galleries as were more than ten feet above the level of the bottom of the shaft. The deep workings would be full, the main galleries would be full, but in the high workings reached by inclines from the main roads there would be a certain amount of air cut off, so to speak, by the water and squeezed up by it. The little science-primers explain how water behaves when you pour it down test-tubes. The flooding of Twenty-Two was an illustration on a large scale.

'By the Holy Grove, what has happened to the air?' It was a Sonthal gangman of Gang Mogul in Number Nine gallery, and he was driving a six-foot way through the coal. Then there was a rush from the other galleries, and Gang Janki and Gang Rahim stumbled up with their basket-women.

'Water has come in the mine,' they said, 'and there is no way of getting out.'

'I went down,' said Janki—'down the slope of my gallery, and I felt the water.'

'There has been no water in the cutting in our time,' clamoured the women. 'Why cannot we go away.'

'Be silent!' said Janki. 'Long ago, when my father was here, water came to Ten—no, Eleven—cutting, and there was great trouble. Let us get away to where the air is better.'

The three gangs and the basket-women left Number Nine gallery and went farther up Number Sixteen. At one turn of the road they could see the pitchy black water lapping on the coal. It had touched the roof of a gallery that they knew well—a gallery where they used to smoke their pipes and manage their flirtations. Seeing this, they called aloud upon their Gods, and the Mehas, who are thrice bastard Mohammedans, strove to recollect the name of the Prophet. They came to a great open square whence nearly all the coal had been extracted. It was the end of the outworkings, and the end of the mine.

Far away down the gallery a small pumping-engine, used for keeping dry a deep working and fed with steam from above, was throbbing faithfully. They heard it cease.

'They have cut off the steam,' said Kundoo hopefully. 'They have given the order to use all the steam for the pit-bank pumps. They will clear out the water.'

'If the water has reached the smoking-gallery,' said Janki, 'all the Company's pumps can do nothing for three days.'

'It is very hot,' moaned Jasoda, the Meah basket-woman. 'There is a very bad air here because of the lamps.'

'Put them out,' said Janki. 'Why do you want lamps?' The lamps were put out, and the company sat still in the utter dark. Somebody rose quietly and began walking over the coals. It was Janki, who was touching the walls with his hands. 'Where is the ledge?' he murmured to himself.

'Sit, sit!' said Kundoo. 'If we die, we die. The air is very bad.'

But Janki still stumbled and crept and tapped with his pick upon the walls. The women rose to their feet.

'Stay all where you are. Without the lamps you cannot see, and I—I am always seeing,' said Janki. Then he paused, and called out: 'O you who have been in the cutting more than ten years, what is the name of this open place? I am an old man and I have forgotten.'

'Bullia's Room,' answered the Sonthal who had complained of the vileness of the air.

'Again,' said Janki.

'Bullia's Room.'

'Then I have found it,' said Janki. 'The name only had slipped my memory. Tibu's gang's gallery is here.'

'A lie,' said Kundoo. 'There have been no galleries in this place since my day.'

'Three paces was the depth of the ledge,' muttered Janki without heeding—'and—oh, my poor bones!—I have found it! It is here, up this ledge. Come all you, one by one, to the place of my voice, and I will count you.'

There was a rush in the dark, and Janki felt the first man's face hit his knees as the Sonthal scrambled up the ledge.

'Who?' cried Janki.

'I, Sunua Manji.'

'Sit you down,' said Janki. 'Who next?'

One by one the women and the men crawled up the ledge which ran along one side of 'Bullia's Room.' Degraded Mohammedan, pig-eating Musahr, and wild Sonthal, Janki ran his hand over them all.

'Now follow after,' said he, 'catching hold of my heel, and the women catching the men's clothes.' He did not ask whether the men had brought their picks with them. A miner, black or white, does not drop his pick. One by one, Janki leading, they crept into the old gallery—a six-foot way with a scant four feet from thill to roof.

'The air is better here,' said Jasoda. They could hear her heart beating in thick, sick bumps.

'Slowly, slowly,' said Janki. 'I am an old man, and I forget many things. This is Tibu's gallery, but where are the four bricks where they used to put their hookah fire on when the Sahibs never saw? Slowly, slowly, O you people behind.'

They heard his hands disturbing the small coal on the floor of the gallery and then a dull sound. 'This is one unbaked brick, and this is another and another. Kundoo is a young man—let him come forward. Put a knee upon this brick and strike here. When Tibu's gang were at dinner on the last day before the good coal ended, they heard the men of Five on the other side, and Five worked their gallery two Sundays later—or it may have been one. Strike there, Kundoo, but give me room to go back.'

Kundoo, doubting, drove the pick, but the first soft crush of the coal was a call to him. He was fighting for his life and for Unda—pretty little Unda with rings on all her toes—for Unda and the forty rupees. The women sang the Song of the Pick—the terrible, slow, swinging melody with the muttered chorus that repeats the sliding of the loosened coal, and, to each cadence, Kundoo smote in the black dark. When he could do no more, Sunua Manji took the pick, and struck for his life and his wife, and his village beyond the blue hills over the Tarachunda River. An hour the men worked, and then the women cleared away the coal.

'It is farther than I thought,' said Janki. 'The air is very bad; but strike, Kundoo, strike hard.'

For the fifth time Kundoo took up the pick as the Sonthal crawled back. The song had scarcely recommenced when it was broken by a yell from Kundoo that echoed down the gallery: 'Par hua! Par hua! We are through, we are through!' The imprisoned air in the mine shot through the opening, and the women at the far end of the gallery heard the water rush through the pillars of 'Bullia's Room' and roar against the ledge. Having fulfilled the law under which it worked, it rose no farther. The women screamed and pressed forward. 'The water has come—we shall be killed! Let us go.'

Kundoo crawled through the gap and found himself in a propped gallery by the simple process of hitting his head against a beam.

'Do I know the pits or do I not?' chuckled Janki. 'This is the Number Five; go you out slowly, giving me your names. Ho, Rahim! count your gang! Now let us go forward, each catching hold of the other as before.'

They formed line in the darkness and Janki led them—for a pitman in a strange pit is only one degree less liable to err than an ordinary mortal underground for the first time. At last they saw a flare-lamp, and Gangs Janki, Mogul, and Rahim of Twenty-two stumbled dazed into the glare of the draught-furnace at the bottom of Five: Janki feeling his way and the rest behind.

'Water has come into Twenty-Two. God knows where are the others. I have brought these men from Tibu's gallery in our cutting, making connection through the north side of the gallery. Take us to the cage,' said Janki Meah.

At the pit-bank of Twenty-Two some thousand people clamoured and wept and shouted. One hundred men—one thousand men— had been drowned in the cutting. They would all go to their homes to-morrow. Where were their men? Little Unda, her cloth drenched with the rain, stood at the pit-mouth calling down the shaft for Kundoo. They had swung the cages clear of the mouth, and her only answer was the murmur of the flood in the pit's-eye two hundred and sixty feet below.
'Look after that woman! She'll chuck herself down the shaft in a minute,' shouted the Manager.

But he need not have troubled; Unda was afraid of death. She wanted Kundoo. The Assistant was watching the flood and seeing how far he could wade into it. There was a lull in the water, and the whirlpool had slackened. The mine was full, and the people at the pit-bank howled.

'My faith, we shall be lucky if we have five hundred hands on the place to-morrow!' said the Manager. 'There's some chance yet of

50

running a temporary dam across that water. Shove in anything-tubs and bullock-carts if you haven't enough bricks. Make them work now if they never worked before. Hi! you gangers! make them work.'

Little by little the crowd was broken into detachments, and pushed towards the water with promises of overtime. The dam-making began, and when it was fairly under way, the Manager thought that the hour had come for the pumps. There was no fresh inrush into the mine. The tall, red, iron-clamped pump-beam rose and fell, and the pumps snored and guttered and shrieked as the first water poured out of the pipe.

'We must run her all to-night,' said the Manager wearily, 'but there's no hope for the poor devils down below. Look here, Gur Sahai, if you are proud of your engines, show me what they can do now.'

Gur Sahai grinned and nodded, with his right hand upon the lever and an oil-can in his left. He could do no more than he was doing, but he could keep that up till the dawn. Were the Company's pumps to be beaten by the vagaries of that troublesome Tarachunda River? Never, never! And the pumps sobbed and panted: 'Never, never!' The Manager sat in the shelter of the pit-bank roofing, trying to dry himself by the pump-boiler fire, and, in the dreary dusk, he saw the crowds on the dam scatter and fly.

'That's the end,' he groaned. ''Twill take us six weeks to persuade 'em that we haven't tried to drown their mates on purpose. Oh for a decent, rational Geordie!'

But the flight had no panic in it. Men had run over from Five with astounding news, and the foremen could not hold their gangs together. Presently, surrounded by a clamorous crew, Gangs Rahim, Mogul, and Janki, and ten basket-women, walked up to report

51

themselves, and pretty little Unda stole away to Janki's hut to prepare his evening meal.

'Alone I found the way,' explained Janki Meah, 'and now will the Company give me pension?'

The simple pit-folk shouted and leaped and went back to the dam, reassured in their old belief that, whatever happened, so great was the power of the Company whose salt they ate, none of them could be killed. But Gur Sahai only bared his white teeth, and kept his hand upon the lever and proved his pumps to the uttermost.

'I say,' said the Assistant to the Manager, a week later, 'do you recollect Germinal?'

'Yes. Queer thing. I thought of it in the cage when that balk went by. Why?'

'Oh, this business seems to be Germinal upsidedown. Janki was in my veranda all this morning, telling me that Kundoo had eloped with his wife—Unda or Anda, I think her name was.'

'Hillo! And those were the cattle you risked your life for to clear out of Twenty-Two!'

'No—I was thinking of the Company's props, not the Company's men.'

'Sounds better to say so now; but I don't believe you, old fellow.'

In Flood Time

Tweed said tae Till:
'What gars ye rin sae still?

52

Till said tae Tweed
'Though ye rin wi' speed
An' I rin slaw—
Yet where ye droon ae man
I droon twa.'

There is no getting over the river to-night, Sahib. They say that a bullock-cart has been washed down already, and the ekka that went over a half-hour before you came has not yet reached the far side. Is the Sahib in haste? I will drive the ford-elephant in to show him. Ohé, mahout there in the shed! Bring out Ram Pershad, and if he will face the current, good. An elephant never lies, Sahib, and Ram Pershad is separated from his friend Kala Nag. He, too, wishes to cross to the far side. Well done! Well done! my King Go half-way across, mahoutji, and see what the river says. Well done, Ram Pershad! Pearl among elephants, go into the river! Hit him on the head, fool! Was the goad made only to scratch thine own fat back with, bastard? Strike strike! What are the boulders to thee, Ram Pershad, my Rustum, my mountain of strength? Go in! Go in!

No, Sahib! It is useless. You can hear him trumpet. He is telling Kala Nag that he cannot come over. See! He has swung round and is shaking his head. He is no fool. He knows what the Barhwi means when it is angry. Aha! Indeed, thou art no fool, my child! Salaam, Ram Pershad, Bahadur! Take him under the trees, mahout, and see that he gets his spices. Well done, thou chiefest among tuskers! Salaam to the Sirkar and go to sleep.

What is to be done? The Sahib must wait till the river goes down. It will shrink to-morrow morning, if God pleases, or the day after at the latest! Now why does the Sahib get so angry? I am his servant. Before God, I did not create this stream! What can I do? My hut and all that is therein is at the service of the Sahib, and it is beginning to rain. Come away, my Lord. How will the river go down for your throwing abuse at it? In the old days the English people were not thus. The fire-carriage has made them soft. In the old days, when

53

they drave behind horses by day or by night, they said naught if a river barred the way, or a carriage sat down in the mud. It was the will of God—not like a fire-carriage which goes and goes and goes, and would go though all the devils in the land hung on to its tail. The fire-carriage hath spoiled the English people. After all, what is a day lost, or, for that matter, what are two days? Is the Sahib going to his own wedding, that he is so mad with haste? Ho! ho! ho! I am an old man and see few Sahibs. Forgive me if I have forgotten the respect that is due to them. The Sahib is not angry?

His own wedding! Ho! ho! ho! The mind of an old man is like the numah-tree. Fruit, bud, blossom, and the dead leaves of all the years of the past flourish together. Old and new and that which is gone out of remembrance, all three are there! Sit on the bedstead, Sahib, and drink milk. Or—would the Sahib in truth care to drink my tobacco? It is good. It is the tobacco of Nuklao. My son, who is in service there, sends it to me. Drink, then, Sahib, if you know how to handle the tube. The Sahib takes it like a Mussulman. Wah! Wah! Where did he learn that? His own wedding! Ho! ho! ho! The Sahib says that there is no wedding in the matter at all. Now is it likely that the Sahib would speak true talk to me who am only a black man? Small wonder, then, that he is in haste. Thirty years have I beaten the gong at this ford, but never have I seen a Sahib in such haste. Thirty years, Sahib! That is a very long time. Thirty years ago this ford was on the track of the bunjaras, and I have seen two thousand pack-bullocks cross in one night. Now the rail has come, and the fire-carriage says buz-buz-buz, and a hundred lakhs of maunds slide across that big bridge. It is very wonderful; but the ford is lonely now that there are no bunjaras to camp under the trees.

Nay, do not trouble to look at the sky without.

It will rain till the dawn. Listen! The boulders are talking to-night in the bed of the river. Hear them! They would be husking your bones, Sahib, had you tried to cross. See, I will shut the door and no rain can enter. Wahi! Ahi! Ugh! Thirty years on the banks of the ford. An old man am I and—where is the oil for the lamp?

Your pardon, but, because of my years, I sleep no sounder than a dog; and you moved to the door. Look then, Sahib. Look and listen. A full half koss from bank to bank is the stream now—you can see it under the stars—and there are ten feet of water therein. It will not shrink because of the anger in your eyes, and it will not be quiet on account of your curses. Which is louder, Sahib—your voice or the voice of the river? Call to it—perhaps it will be ashamed. Lie down and sleep afresh, Sahib. I know the anger of the Barhwi when there has fallen rain in the foot-hills. I swam the flood, once, on a night tenfold worse than this, and by the Favour of God I was released from Death when I had come to the very gates thereof.
May I tell the tale? Very good talk. I will fill the pipe anew.

Thirty years ago it was, when I was a young man and had but newly come to the ford. I was strong then, and the bunjaras had no doubt when I said: 'This ford is clear.' I have toiled all night up to my shoulder-blades in running water amid a hundred bullocks mad with fear, and have brought them across losing not a hoof. When all was done I fetched the shivering men, and they gave me for reward the pick of their cattle—the bell-bullock of the drove. So great was the honour in which I was held! But to-day, when the rain falls and the river rises, I creep into my hut and whimper like a dog. My strength is gone from me. I am an old man and the fire-carriage has made the ford desolate. They were wont to call me the Strong One of the Barhwi.

Behold my face, Sahib—it is the face of a monkey. And my arm—it is the arm of an old woman. I swear to you, Sahib, that a woman has loved this face and has rested in the hollow of this arm. Twenty years ago, Sahib. Believe me, this was true talk—twenty years ago.

Come to the door and look across. Can you see a thin fire very far away down the stream? That is the temple-fire, in the shrine of

Hanuman, of the village of Pateera. North, under the big star, is the village itself, but it is hidden by a bend of the river. Is that far to swim, Sahib? Would you take off your clothes and adventure? Yet I swam to Pateera—not once, but many times; and there are muggers in the river too.

Love knows no caste; else why should I, a Mussulman and the son of a Mussulman, have sought a Hindu woman—a widow of the Hindus—the sister of the headman of Pateera? But it was even so. They of the headman's household came on a pilgrimage to Muttra when She was but newly a bride. Silver tyres were upon the wheels of the bullock-cart, and silken curtains hid the woman. Sahib, I made no haste in their conveyance, for the wind parted the curtains and I saw Her. When they returned from pilgrimage the boy that was Her husband had died, and I saw Her again in the bullock-cart. By God, these Hindus are fools! What was it to me whether She was Hindu or Jain—scavenger, leper, or whole? I would have married Her and made Her a home by the ford. The Seventh of the Nine Bars says that a man may not marry one of the idolaters? Is that truth? Both Shiahs and Sunnis say that a Mussulman may not marry one of the idolaters? Is the Sahib a priest, then, that he knows so much? I will tell him something that he does not know. There is neither Shiah nor Sunni, forbidden nor idolater, in Love; and the Nine Bars are but nine little faggots that the flame of Love utterly burns away. In truth, I would have taken Her; but what could I do? The headman would have sent his men to break my head with staves. I am not—I was not—afraid of any five men; but against half a village who can prevail?

Therefore it was my custom, these things having been arranged between us twain, to go by night to the village of Pateera, and there we met among the crops, no man knowing aught of the matter. Behold, now! I was wont to cross here, skirting the jungle to the river bend where the railway bridge is, and thence across the elbow of land to Pateera. The light of the shrine was my guide when the nights were dark. That jungle near the river is very full of snakes—

little karaits that sleep on the sand—and moreover, Her brothers would have slain me had they found me in the crops. But none knew—none knew save She and I; and the blown sand of the river-bed covered the track of my feet. In the hot months it was an easy thing to pass from the ford to Pateera, and in the first Rains, when the river rose slowly, it was an easy thing also. I set the strength of my body against the strength of the stream, and nightly I ate in my hut here and drank at Pateera yonder. She had said that one Hirnam Singh, a thief, had sought Her, and he was of a village up the river but on the same bank. All Sikhs are dogs, and they have refused in their folly that good gift of God—tobacco. I was ready to destroy Hirnam Singh that ever he had come nigh Her; and the more because he had sworn to Her that She had a lover, and that he would lie in wait and give the name to the headman unless She went away with him. What curs are these Sikhs!

After that news I swam always with a little sharp knife in my belt, and evil would it have been for a man had he stayed me. I knew not the face of Hirnam Singh, but I would have killed any who came between me and Her.

Upon a night in the beginning of the Rains I was minded to go across to Pateera, albeit the river was angry. Now the nature of the Barhwi is this, Sahib. In twenty breaths it comes down from the Hills a wall three feet high, and I have seen it, between the lighting of a fire and the cooking of a cake, grow from a runnel to a sister of the Jumna.

When I left this bank there was a shoal a half-mile down, and I made shift to fetch it and draw breath there ere going forward; for I felt the hands of the river heavy upon my heels. Yet what will a young man not do for Love's sake? There was but little light from the stars, and midway to the shoal a branch of the stinking deodar tree brushed my mouth as I swam. That was a sign of heavy rain in the foot-hills and beyond, for the deodar is a strong tree, not easily shaken from the hillsides. I made haste, the river aiding me, but ere

I had touched the shoal, the pulse of the stream beat, as it were, within me and around, and, behold, the shoal was gone and I rode high on the crest of a wave that ran from bank to bank. Has the Sahib ever been cast into much water that fights and will not let a man use his limbs? To me, my head upon the water, it seemed as though there were naught but water to the world's end, and the river drave me with its driftwood. A man is a very little thing in the belly of a flood. And this flood, though I knew it not, was the Great Flood about which men talk still. My liver was dissolved and I lay like a log upon my back in the fear of Death. There were living things in the water, crying and howling grievously—beasts of the forest and cattle, and once the voice of a man asking for help. But the rain came and lashed the water white, and I heard no more save the roar of the boulders below and the roar of the rain above. Thus I was whirled downstream, wrestling for the breath in me. It is very hard to die when one is young. Can the Sahib, standing here, see the railway bridge? Look, there are the lights of the mail-train going to Peshawur! The bridge is now twenty feet above the river, but upon that night the water was roaring against the lattice-work, and against the lattice came I feet first. But much driftwood was piled there and upon the piers, and I took no great hurt. Only the river pressed me as a strong man presses a weaker. Scarcely could I take hold of the lattice-work and crawl to the upper boom. Sahib, the water was foaming across the rails a foot deep! Judge therefore what manner of flood it must have been. I could not hear. I could not see. I could but lie on the boom and pant for breath.

After a while the rain ceased and there came out in the sky certain new-washed stars, and by their light I saw that there was no end to the black water as far as the eye could travel, and the water had risen upon the rails. There were dead beasts in the driftwood on the piers, and others caught by the neck in the lattice-work, and others not yet drowned who strove to find a foothold on the lattice-work-buffaloes and kine, and wild pig, and deer one or two, and snakes and jackals past all counting. Their bodies were black upon the left side of the bridge, but the smaller of them were forced through the lattice-work and whirled down-stream.

Thereafter the stars died and the rain came down afresh and the river rose yet more, and I felt the bridge begin to stir under me as a man stirs in his sleep ere he wakes. But I was not afraid, Sahib. I swear to you that I was not afraid, though I had no power in my limbs. I knew that I should not die till I had seen Her once more. But I was very cold, and I felt that the bridge must go.

There was a trembling in the water, such a trembling as goes before the coming of a great wave, and the bridge lifted its flank to the rush of that coming so that the right lattice dipped under water and the left rose clear. On my beard, Sahib, I am speaking God's truth! As a Mirzapore stone-boat careens to the wind, so the Barhwi Bridge turned. Thus and in no other manner.

I slid from the boom into deep water, and behind me came the wave of the wrath of the river. I heard its voice and the scream of the middle part of the bridge as it moved from the piers and sank, and I knew no more till I rose in the middle of the great flood. I put forth my hand to swim, and lo! it fell upon the knotted hair of the head of a man. He was dead, for no one but I, the Strong One of Barhwi, could have lived in that race. He had been dead full two days, for he rode high, wallowing, and was an aid to me. I laughed then, knowing for a surety that I should yet see Her and take no harm; and I twisted my fingers in the hair of the man, for I was far spent, and together we went down the stream—he the dead and I the living. Lacking that help I should have sunk: the cold was in my marrow, and my flesh was ribbed and sodden on my bones. But he had no fear who had known the uttermost of the power of the river; and I let him go where he chose. At last we came into the power of a side-current that set to the right bank, and I strove with my feet to draw with it. But the dead man swung heavily in the whirl, and I feared that some branch had struck him and that he would sink. The tops of the tamarisks brushed my knees, so I knew we were come into flood-water above the crops, and, after, I let down my legs and felt bottom—the ridge of a field—and, after, the dead man stayed upon a knoll under a fig-tree, and I drew my body from the water rejoicing.

Does the Sahib know whither the backwash of the flood had borne me? To the knoll which is the eastern boundary-mark of the village of Pateera! No other place. I drew the dead man up on the grass for the service that he had done me, and also because I knew not whether I should need him again. Then I went, crying thrice like a jackal, to the appointed place, which was near the byre of the headman's house. But my Love was already there, weeping. She feared that the flood had swept my hut at the Barhwi Ford. When I came softly through the ankle-deep water, She thought it was a ghost and would have fled, but I put my arms round Her, and—I was no ghost in those days, though I am an old man now. Ho! ho! Dried corn, in truth. Maize without juice. Ho! ho!

I told Her the story of the breaking of the Barhwi Bridge, and She said that I was greater than mortal man, for none may cross the Barhwi in full flood, and I had seen what never man had seen before. Hand in hand we went to the knoll where the dead lay, and I showed Her by what help I had made the ford. She looked also upon the body under the stars, for the latter end of the night was clear, and hid Her face in Her hands, crying: 'It is the body of Hirnam Singh!' I said: 'The swine is of more use dead than living, my Beloved,' and She said: 'Surely, for he has saved the dearest life in the world to my love. None the less, he cannot stay here, for that would bring shame upon me.' The body was not a gunshot from Her door.

Then said I, rolling the body with my hands 'God hath judged between us, Hirnam Singh, that thy blood might not be upon my head. Now, whether I have done thee a wrong in keeping thee from the burning-ghat, do thou and the crows settle together.' So I cast him adrift into the flood-water, and he was drawn out to the open, ever wagging his thick black beard like a priest under the pulpit-board. And I saw no more of Hirnam Singh.

Before the breaking of the day we two parted, and I moved towards such of the jungle as was not flooded. With the full light I saw what I had done in the darkness, and the bones of my body were loosened in my flesh, for there ran two koss of raging water between the village of Pateera and the trees of the far bank, and, in the middle, the piers of the Barhwi Bridge showed like broken teeth in the jaw of an old man. Nor was there any life upon the waters—neither birds nor boats, but only an army of drowned things—bullocks and horses and men—and the river was redder than blood from the clay of the foot-hills. Never had I seen such a flood—never since that year have I seen the like—and, O Sahib, no man living had done what I had done. There was no return for me that day. Not for all the lands of the headman would I venture a second time without the shield of darkness that cloaks danger. I went a koss up the river to the house of a blacksmith, saying that the flood had swept me from my hut, and they gave me food. Seven days I stayed with the blacksmith, till a boat came and I returned to my house. There was no trace of wall, or roof, or floor—naught but a patch of slimy mud. Judge, therefore, Sahib, how far the river must have risen.

It was written that I should not die either in my house, or in the heart of the Barhwi, or under the wreck of the Barhwi Bridge, for God sent down Hirnam Singh two days dead, though I know not how the man died, to be my buoy and support. Hirnam Singh has been in Hell these twenty years, and the thought of that night must be the flower of his torment.

Listen, Sahib! The river has changed its voice. It is going to sleep before the dawn, to which there is yet one hour. With the light it will come down afresh. How do I know? Have I been here thirty years without knowing the voice of the river as a father knows the voice of his son? Every moment it is talking less angrily. I swear that ere will be no danger for one hour or, perhaps, two. I cannot

61

answer for the morning. Be quick, Sahib! I will call Ram Pershad, and he will not turn back this time. Is the paulin tightly corded upon all the baggage? Ohé, mahout with a mud head, the elephant for the Sahib, and tell them on the far side that there will be no crossing after daylight.

Money? Nay, Sahib. I am not of that kind. No, not even to give sweetmeats to the baby-folk. My house, look you, is empty, and I am an old man.

Dutt, Ram Pershad! Dutt! Dutt! Dutt! Good luck go with you, Sahib.

The Sending of Dana Da

Once upon a time, some people in India made a new Heaven and a new Earth out of broken teacups, a missing brooch or two, and a hairbrush. These were hidden under bushes, or stuffed into holes in the hillside, and an entire Civil Service of subordinate Gods used to find or mend them again; and every one said: 'There are more things in Heaven and Earth than are dreamt of in our philosophy.' Several other things happened also, but the Religion never seemed to get much beyond its first manifestations; though it added an air-line postal service and orchestral effects in order to keep abreast of the times and choke off competition.

This Religion was too elastic for ordinary use. It stretched itself and embraced pieces of everything that the medicine-men of all ages have manufactured. It approved of and stole from Freemasonry; looted the Latter-day Rosicrucians of half their pet words; took any fragments of Egyptian philosophy that it found in the Encyclopædia Britannica; annexed as many of the Vedas as had been translated into French or English, and talked of all the rest; built in the German versions of what is left of the Zend Avesta; encouraged White, Grey, and Black Magic, including spiritualism, palmistry, fortune-telling by cards, hot chestnuts, double-kernelled nuts, and tallow droppings; would have adopted Voodoo and Obeah had it known anything about them, and showed itself, in every way, one of the most accommodating arrangements that had ever been invented since the birth of the Sea.

When it was in thorough working order, with all the machinery, down to the subscriptions, complete, Dana Da came from nowhere, with nothing in his hands, and wrote a chapter in its history which has hitherto been unpublished. He said that his first name was Dana, and his second was Da. Now, setting aside Dana of the New York Sun, Dana is a Bhil name, and Da fits no native of India unless you accept the Bengali De as the original spelling. Da is Lap or Finnish; and Dana Da was neither Finn, Chin, Bhil, Bengali, Lap, Nair, Gond, Romany, Magh, Bokhariot, Kurd, Armenian, Levantine, Jew, Persian, Punjabi, Madrasi, Parsee, nor anything else known to ethnologists. He was simply Dana Da, and declined to give further information. For the sake of brevity and as roughly indicating his origin, he was called 'The Native.' He might have been the original Old Man of the Mountains, who is said to be the only authorised Head of the Tea-cup Creed. Some people said that he was; but Dana Da used to smile and deny any connection with the cult, explaining that he was an 'Independent Experimenter.'

As I have said, he came from nowhere, with his hands behind his back, and studied the Creed for three weeks, sitting at the feet of those best competent to explain its mysteries. Then he laughed aloud and went away, but the laugh might have been either of devotion or derision.

When he returned he was without money, but his pride was unabated. He declared that he knew more about the Things in Heaven and Earth than those who taught him, and for this contumacy was abandoned altogether.

His next appearance in public life was at a big cantonment in Upper India, and he was then telling fortunes with the help of three leaden dice, a very dirty old cloth, and a little tin box of opium pills. He told better fortunes when he was allowed half a bottle of whisky; but the things which he invented on the opium were quite worth the money. He was in reduced circumstances. Among other people's he told the fortune of an Englishman who had once been interested in the Simla Creed, but who, later on, had married and forgotten all his old knowledge in the study of babies and things. The Englishman allowed Dana Da to tell a fortune for 'charity's sake, and gave him five rupees, a dinner, and some old clothes. When he had eaten, Dana Da professed gratitude, and asked if there were anything he could do for his host—in the esoteric line.

'Is there any one that you love?' said Dana Da. The Englishman loved his wife, but had no desire to drag her name into the conversation. He therefore shook his head.

'Is there any one that you hate?' said Dana Da. The Englishman said that there were several men whom he hated deeply.

'Very good,' said Dana Da, upon whom the whisky and the opium were beginning to tell. 'Only give me their names, and I will despatch a Sending to them and kill them.'

Now a Sending is a horrible arrangement, first invented, they say, in Iceland. It is a Thing sent by a wizard, and may take any form, but, most generally, wanders about the land in the shape of a little purple cloud till it finds the Sendee, and him it kills by changing into the form of a horse, or a cat, or a man without a face. It is not strictly a native patent, though chamars of the skin and hide castes can, if irritated, despatch a Sending which sits on the breast of their enemy by night and nearly kills him. Very few natives care to irritate chamars for this reason.

'Let me despatch a Sending,' said Dana Da. 'I am nearly dead now with want, and drink, and opium; but I should like to kill a man before I die. I can send a Sending anywhere you choose, and in any form except in the shape of a man.'

The Englishman had no friends that he wished to kill, but partly to soothe Dana Da, whose eyes were rolling, and partly to see what would be done, he asked whether a modified Sending could not be arranged for—such a Sending as should make a man's life a burden to him, and yet do him no harm. If this were possible, he notified his willingness to give Dana Da ten rupees for the job.

'I am not what I was once,' said Dana Da, 'and I must take the money because I am poor. To what Englishman shall I send it?'

'Send a Sending to Lone Sahib,' said the Englishman, naming a man who had been most bitter in rebuking him for his apostasy from the Tea-cup Creed. Dana Da laughed and nodded.

'I could have chosen no better man myself,' said he. 'I will see that he finds the Sending about his path and about his bed.'

He lay down on the hearth-rug, turned up the whites of his eyes, shivered all over, and began to snort. This was Magic, or Opium, or the Sending, or all three. When he opened his eyes he vowed that the Sending had started upon the war-path, and was at that moment flying up to the town where Lone Sahib lived.

'Give me my ten rupees,' said Dana Da wearily, 'and write a letter to Lone Sahib, telling him, and all who believe with him, that you and a friend are using a power greater than theirs. They will see that you are speaking the truth.'

He departed unsteadily, with the promise of some more rupees if anything came of the Sending.

The Englishman sent a letter to Lone Sahib, couched in what he remembered of the terminology of the Creed. He wrote: 'I also, in the days of what you held to be my backsliding, have obtained Enlightenment, and with Enlightenment has come Power.' Then he grew so deeply, mysterious that the recipient of the letter could make neither head nor tail of it, and was proportionately impressed; for he fancied that his friend had become a 'fifth-rounder.' When a man is a 'fifth-rounder' he can do more than Slade and Houdin combined.

Lone Sahib read the letter in five different fashions, and was beginning a sixth interpretation when his bearer dashed in with the news that there was a cat on the bed. Now if there was one thing that Lone Sahib hated more than another, it was a cat. He scolded the bearer for not turning it out of the house. The bearer said that he was afraid. All the doors of the bedroom had been shut throughout the morning, and no real cat could possibly have entered the room. He would prefer not to meddle with the creature.

Lone Sahib entered the room gingerly, and there, on the pillow of his bed, sprawled and whimpered a wee white kitten; not a jumpsome, frisky little beast, but a slug-like crawler with its eyes barely opened and its paws lacking strength or direction—a kitten that ought to have been in a basket with its mamma. Lone Sahib caught it by the scruff of its neck, handed it over to the sweeper to be drowned, and fined the bearer four annas.

That evening, as he was reading in his room, he fancied that he saw something moving about on the hearth-rug, outside the circle of light from his reading-lamp. When the thing began to myowl he realised that it was a kitten—a wee white kitten, nearly blind and very miserable.

He was seriously angry, and spoke bitterly to his bearer, who said that there was no kitten in the room when he brought in the lamp, and real kittens of tender age generally had mother-cats in attendance.

'If the Presence will go out into the veranda and listen,' said the bearer, 'he will hear no cats. How, therefore, can the kitten on the bed and the kitten on the hearth-rug be real kittens?'

Lone Sahib went out to listen, and the bearer followed him, but there was no sound of any one mewing for her children. He returned to his room, having hurled the kitten down the hillside, and wrote out the incidents of the day for the benefit of his co-religionists. Those people were so absolutely free from superstition that they ascribed anything a little out of the common to Agencies. As it was their business to know all about the Agencies, they were on terms of almost indecent familiarity with Manifestations of every kind. Their letters dropped from the ceiling—unstamped—and Spirits used to squatter up and down their staircases all night; but they had never come into contact with kittens. Lone Sahib wrote out the facts, noting the hour and the minute, as every Psychical Observer is bound to do, and appending the Englishman's letter, because it was the most mysterious document and might have had a bearing upon anything in this world or the next. An outsider would have translated all the tangle thus: 'Look out! You laughed at me once, and now I am going to make you sit up.'

Lone Sahib's co-religionists found that meaning in it; but their translation was refined and full of four-syllable words. They held a sederunt, and were filled with tremulous joy, for, in spite of their familiarity with all the other worlds and cycles, they had a very human awe of things sent from Ghostland. They met in Lone Sahib's room in shrouded and sepulchral gloom, and their conclave was broken up by a clinking among the photo-frames on the mantelpiece. A wee white kitten, nearly blind, was looping and writhing itself between the clock and the candlesticks. That stopped all investigations or doubtings. Here was the Manifestation in the flesh. It was, so far as could be seen, devoid of purpose, but it was a Manifestation of undoubted authenticity.

They drafted a Round Robin to the Englishman; the backslider of old days, adjuring him in the interests of the Creed to explain whether there was any connection between the embodiment of some Egyptian God or other (I have forgotten the name) and his communication. They called the kitten Ra, or Thoth, or Tum, or something; and when Lone Sahib confessed that the first one had, at his most misguided instance, been drowned by the sweeper, they said consolingly that in his next life he would be a 'bounder,' and not even a 'rounder' of the lowest grade. These words may not be quite correct, but they accurately express the sense of the house.

When the Englishman received the Round Robin—it came by post— he was startled and bewildered. He sent into the bazar for Dana Da, who read the letter and laughed. 'That is my Sending,' said he. 'I told you I would work well. Now give me another ten rupees.'

'But what in the world is this gibberish about Egyptian Gods?' asked the Englishman.

'Cats,' said Dana Da with a hiccough, for he had discovered the Englishman's whisky-bottle. 'Cats, and cats, and cats! Never was such a Sending. A hundred of cats. Now give me ten more rupees and write as I dictate.'

Dana Da's letter was a curiosity. It bore the Englishman's signature, and hinted at cats—at a Sending of Cats. The mere words on paper were creepy and uncanny to behold.

'What have you done, though?' said the Englishman. 'I am as much in the dark as ever. Do you mean to say that you can actually send this absurd Sending you talk about?'

'Judge for yourself,' said Dana Da. 'What does that letter mean? In a little time they will all be at my feet and yours, and I—oh, glory!—will be drugged or drunk all day long.'

Dana Da knew his people.

When a man who hates cats wakes up in the morning and finds a little squirming kitten on his breast, or puts his hand into his ulster-pocket and finds a little half-dead kitten where his gloves should be, or opens his trunk and finds a vile kitten among his dress-shirts, or goes for a long ride with his mackintosh strapped on his saddlebow and shakes a little squawling kitten from its folds when he opens it, or goes out to dinner and finds a little blind kitten under his chair, or stays at home and finds a writhing kitten under the quilt, or wriggling among his boots, or hanging, head downwards, in his tobacco jar, or being mangled by his terrier in the veranda,—when such a man finds one kitten, neither more nor less, once a day in a place where no kitten rightly could or should be, he is naturally upset. When he dare not murder his daily trove because he believes it to be a Manifestation, an Emissary, an Embodiment, and half-a-dozen other things all out of the regular course of nature, he is more than upset. He is actually distressed. Some of Lone Sahib's co-religionists thought that he was a highly-favoured individual; but many said that if he had treated the first kitten with proper respect—as suited a Thoth-Ra-Tum-Sennacherib Embodiment—all this trouble would have been averted. They compared him to the Ancient Mariner, but none the less they were proud of him and proud of the Englishman who had sent the Manifestation. They did not call it a Sending because Icelandic magic was not in their programme.

After sixteen kittens, that is to say, after one fortnight, for there were three kittens on the first day to impress the fact of the Sending, the whole camp was uplifted by a letter—it came flying through a window—from the Old Man of the Mountains—the Head of all the Creed—explaining the Manifestation in the most beautiful language and soaking up all the credit of it for himself. The Englishman, said the letter, was not there at all. He was a backslider without Power or Asceticism, who could not even raise a table by force of volition, much less project an army of kittens through space. The entire arrangement, said the letter, was strictly orthodox, worked and sanctioned by the highest Authorities within the pale of the Creed. There was great joy at this, for some of the weaker brethren, seeing that an outsider who had been working on independent lines could create kittens, whereas their own rulers had never gone beyond crockery—and broken at best—were showing a desire to break line on their own trail. In fact, there was the promise of a schism. A second Round Robin was drafted to the Englishman, beginning: 'O Scoffer,' and ending with a selection of curses from the Rites of Mizraim and Memphis, and the Commination of Jugana, who was a 'fifth-rounder' upon whose name an upstart 'third-rounder ' once traded. A papal excommunication is a billet-doux compared with the Commination of Jugana. The Englishman had been proved, under the hand and seal of the Old Man of the Mountains, to have appropriated Virtue and pretended to have Power which, in reality, belonged only to the Supreme Head. Naturally the Round Robin did not spare him.

He handed the letter to Dana Da to translate into decent English. The effect on Dana Da was curious. At first he was furiously angry, and then he laughed for five minutes.

'I had thought,' he said, 'that they would have come to me. In another week I would have shown that I sent the Sending, and, they would have discrowned the Old Man of the Mountains who has sent this Sending of mine. Do you do nothing. The time has come for me to act. Write as I dictate, and I will put them to shame. But give me ten more rupees.'

At Dana Da's dictation the Englishman wrote nothing less than a formal challenge to the Old Man of the Mountains. It wound up: 'And if this Manifestation be from your hand, then let it go forward;

but if it be from my hand, I will that the Sending shall cease in two days' time. On that day there shall be twelve kittens and thenceforward none at all. The people shall judge between us.' This was signed by Dana Da, who added pentacles and pentagrams, and a crux ansata, and half-a-dozen swastikas, and a Triple Tau to his name, just to show that he was all he laid claim to be.

The challenge was read out to the gentlemen and ladies, and they remembered then that Dana Da had laughed at them some years ago. It was officially announced that the Old Man of the Mountains would treat the matter with contempt; Dana Da being an Independent Investigator without a single 'round' at the back of him. But this did not soothe his people. They wanted to see a fight. They were very human for all their spirituality. Lone Sahib, who was really being worn out with kittens, submitted meekly to his fate. He felt that he was being 'kittened to prove the power of Dana Da,' as the poet says.

When the stated day dawned the shower of kittens began. Some were white and some were tabby, and all were about the same loathsome age. Three were on his hearth-rug, three in his bathroom, and the other six turned up at intervals among the visitors who came to see the prophecy break down. Never was a more satisfactory Sending. On the next day there were no kittens, and the next day and all the other days were kittenless and quiet. The people murmured and looked to the Old Man of the Mountains for an explanation. A letter, written on a palm-leaf, dropped from the ceiling, but every one except Lone Sahib felt that letters were not what the occasion demanded. There should have been cats, there should have been cats,—full-grown ones. The letter proved conclusively that there had been a hitch in the Psychic Current which, colliding with a Dual Identity, had interfered with the Percipient Activity all along the main line. The kittens were still going on, but owing to some failure in the Developing Fluid, they were not materialised. The air was thick with letters for a few days afterwards. Unseen hands played Gluck and Beethoven on finger-bowls and clock-shades; but all men felt that Psychic Life was a mockery without materialised kittens. Even Lone Sahib shouted with the majority on this head. Dana Da's letters were very insulting, and if he had then offered to lead a new departure, there is no knowing what might not have happened.

But Dana Da was dying of whisky and opium in the Englishman's godown, and had small heart for honours.

'They have been put to shame,' said he. 'Never was such a Sending. It has killed me.'

'Nonsense!' said the Englishman. 'You are going to die, Dana Da, and that sort of stuff must be left behind. I'll admit that you have made some queer things come about. Tell me honestly, now, how was it done?'

'Give me ten more rupees,' said Dana Da faintly, 'and if I die before I spend them, bury them with me.'

The silver was counted out while Dana Da was fighting with Death. His hand closed upon the money and he smiled a grim smile.

'Bend low,' he whispered. The Englishman bent.

'Bunnia — Mission-school — expelled — boxwallah [peddler] — Ceylon pearl-merchant — all mine English education—out-casted, and made up name Dana Da—England with American thought-reading man and—and—you gave me ten rupees several times—I gave the Sahib's bearer two-eight a month for cats—little, little cats. I wrote—and he put them about—very clever man. Very few kittens now in the bazar. Ask Lone Sahib's sweeper's wife.'

So saying, Dana Da gasped and passed away into a land where, if all be true, there are no materialisations and the making of new creeds is discouraged.

But consider the gorgeous simplicity of it all.

Lalun is a member of the most ancient profession in the world. Lilith was her very-great-grandmamma, and that was before the days of Eve, as every one knows. In the West, people say rude things about Lalun's profession, and write lectures about it, and distribute the lectures to young persons in order that Morality may be preserved. In the East, where the profession is hereditary, descending from mother to daughter, nobody writes lectures or takes any notice; and that is a distinct proof of the inability of the East to manage its own affairs.

Lalun's real husband, for even ladies of Lalun's profession in the East must have husbands, was a big jujube-tree. Her Mamma, who had married a fig-tree, spent ten thousand rupees on Lalun's wedding, which was blessed by forty-seven clergymen of Mamma's Church, and distributed five thousand rupees in charity to the poor. And that was the custom of the land. The advantages of having a jujube-tree for a husband are obvious. You cannot hurt his feelings, and he looks imposing.

Lalun's husband stood on the plain outside the City walls, and Lalun's house was upon the east wall facing the river. If you fell from the broad window-seat you dropped thirty feet sheer into the City Ditch. But if you stayed where you should and looked forth, you saw all the cattle of the City being driven down to water, the students of the Government College playing cricket, the high grass and trees that fringed the river-bank, the great sand-bars that ribbed the river, the red tombs of dead Emperors beyond the river, and very far away through the blue heat-haze a glint of the snows of the Himalayas.

Wali Dad used to lie in the window-seat for hours at a time watching this view. He was a young Mohammedan who was suffering acutely from education of the English variety and knew it. His father had sent him to a Mission-school to get wisdom, and Wali Dad had absorbed more than ever his father or the Missionaries intended he should. When his father died, Wali Dad was independent and spent two years experimenting with the creeds of the Earth and reading books that are of no use to anybody.

After he had made an unsuccessful attempt to enter the Roman Catholic Church and the Presbyterian fold at the same time (the Missionaries found him out and called him names; but they did not understand his trouble), he discovered Lalun on the City wall and became the most constant of her few admirers. He possessed a head that English artists at home would rave over and paint amid impossible surroundings—a face that female novelists would use with delight through nine hundred pages. In reality he was only a clean-bred young Mohammedan, with pencilled eyebrows, small-cut nostrils, little feet and hands, and a very tired look in his eyes. By virtue of his twenty-two years he had grown a neat black beard which he stroked with pride and kept delicately scented. His life seemed to be divided between borrowing books from me and making love to Lalun in the window-seat. He composed songs about her, and some of the songs are sung to this day in the City from the Street of the Mutton-Butchers to the Copper-Smiths' ward.

One song, the prettiest of all, says that the beauty of Lalun was so great that it troubled the hearts of the British Government and caused them to lose their peace of mind. That is the way the song is sung in the streets; but, if you examine it carefully and know the key to the explanation, you will find that there are three puns in it—on 'beauty,' 'heart,' and 'peace of mind,'—so that it runs: 'By the subtlety of Lalun the administration of the Government was troubled and it lost such-and-such a man.' When Wali Dad sings that song his eyes glow like hot coals, and Lalun leans back among the cushions and throws bunches of jasmine-buds at Wali Dad.

But first it is necessary to explain something about the Supreme Government which is above all and below all and behind all. Gentlemen come from England, spend a few weeks in India, walk round this great Sphinx of the Plains, and write books upon its ways and its works, denouncing or praising it as their own ignorance prompts. Consequently all the world knows how the Supreme Government conducts itself. But no one, not even the Supreme Government, knows everything about the administration of the Empire. Year by year England sends out fresh drafts for the first fighting-line, which is officially called the Indian Civil Service. These die, or kill themselves by overwork, or are worried to death, or broken in health and hope in order that the land may be protected from death and sickness, famine and war, and may eventually become capable of standing alone. It will never stand alone, but the idea is a pretty one, and men are willing to die for it, and yearly the work of pushing and coaxing and scolding and petting the country into good living goes forward. If an advance be made all credit is given to the native, while the Englishmen stand back and wipe their foreheads. If a failure occurs the Englishmen step forward and take the blame. Overmuch tenderness of this kind has bred a strong belief among many natives that the native is capable of administering the country, and many devout Englishmen believe this also, because the theory is stated in beautiful English with all the latest political colours.

There are other men who, though uneducated, see visions and dream dreams, and they, too, hope to administer the country in their own way—that is to say, with a garnish of Red Sauce. Such men must exist among two hundred million people, and, if they are not attended to, may cause trouble and even break the great idol called Pax Britannica, which, as the newspapers say, lives between Peshawur and Cape Comorin. Were the Day of Doom to dawn to-morrow, you would find the Supreme Government 'taking measures to allay popular excitement,' and putting guards upon the graveyards that the Dead might troop forth orderly. The youngest Civilian would arrest Gabriel on his own responsibility if the Archangel could not produce a Deputy-Commissioner's permission to 'make music or other noises' as the licence says.

Whence it is easy to see that mere men of the flesh who would create a tumult must fare badly at the hands of the Supreme Government. And they do. There is no outward sign of excitement; there is no confusion; there is no knowledge. When due and sufficient reasons have been given, weighed and approved, the machinery moves forward, and the dreamer of dreams and the seer of visions is gone from his friends and following. He enjoys the hospitality of Government; there is no restriction upon his movements within certain limits; but he must not confer any more with his brother dreamers. Once in every six months the Supreme Government assures itself that he is well and takes formal acknowledgment of his existence. No one protests against his detention, because the few people who know about it are in deadly fear of seeming to know him; and never a single newspaper 'takes up his case' or organises demonstrations on his behalf, because the newspapers of India have got behind that lying proverb which says the Pen is mightier than the Sword, and can walk delicately.

So now you know as much as you ought about Wali Dad, the educational mixture, and the Supreme Government.

Lalun has not yet been described. She would need, so Wali Dad says, a thousand pens of gold, and ink scented with musk. She has been variously compared to the Moon, the Dil Sagar Lake, a spotted quail, a gazelle, the Sun on the Desert of Kutch, the Dawn, the Stars, and the young bamboo. These comparisons imply that she is beautiful exceedingly according to the native standards, which are practically the same as those of the West. Her eyes are black and her hair is black, and her eyebrows are black as leeches; her mouth is tiny and says witty things; her hands are tiny and have saved much money; her feet are tiny and have trodden on the naked hearts of many men. But, as Wali Dad sings: 'Lalun is Lalun, and when you have said that, you have only come to the Beginnings of Knowledge.'

The little house on the City wall was just big enough to hold Lalun, and her maid, and a pussycat with a silver collar. A big pink-and-blue cut-glass chandelier hung from the ceiling of the reception room. A petty Nawab had given Lalun the horror, and she kept it for politeness' sake. The floor of the room was of polished chunam, white as curds. A latticed window of carved wood was set in one wall; there was a profusion of squabby pluffy cushions and fat carpets everywhere, and Lalun's silver hookah, studded with turquoises, had a special little carpet all to its shining self. Wali Dad was nearly as permanent a fixture as the chandelier. As I have said, he lay in the window-seat and meditated on Life and Death and Lalun—'specially Lalun. The feet of the young men of the City tended to her doorways and then—retired, for Lalun was a particular maiden, slow of speech, reserved of mind, and not in the least inclined to orgies which were nearly certain to end in strife. 'If I am of no value, I am unworthy of this honour,' said Lalun. 'If I am of value, they are unworthy of Me.' And that was a crooked sentence.

In the long hot nights of latter April and May all the City seemed to assemble in Lalun's little white room to smoke and to talk. Shiahs of the grimmest and most uncompromising persuasion; Sufis who had lost all belief in the Prophet and retained but little in God; wandering Hindu priests passing southward on their way to the Central India fairs and other affairs; Pundits in black gowns, with spectacles on their noses and undigested wisdom in their insides; bearded headmen of the wards; Sikhs with all the details of the latest ecclesiastical scandal in the Golden Temple; red-eyed priests from beyond the Border, looking like trapped wolves and talking like ravens; M.A.'s of the University, very superior and very voluble—all these people and more also you might find in the white room. Wali Dad lay in the window-seat and listened to the talk.

'It is Lalun's salon,' said Wali Dad to me, 'and it is electic—is not that the word? Outside of a Freemasons' Lodge I have never seen such gatherings. There I dined once with a Jew—a Yahoudi!' He spat into the City Ditch with apologies for allowing national feelings to overcome him. 'Though I have lost every belief in the world,' said he, 'and try to be proud of my losing, I cannot help hating a Jew. Lalun admits no Jews here.'

'But what in the world do all these men do? 'I asked.

'The curse of our country,' said Wali Dad. 'They talk. It is like the Athenians—always hearing and telling some new thing. Ask the Pearl and she will show you how much she knows of the news of the City and the Province. Lalun knows everything.'

'Lalun,' I said at random—she was talking to a gentleman of the Kurd persuasion who had come in from God-knows-where—'when does the 175th Regiment go to Agra?'

'It does not go at all,' said Lalun, without turning her head. 'They have ordered the 118th to go in its stead. That Regiment goes to Lucknow in three months, unless they give a fresh order.'

'That is so,' said Wali Dad, without a shade of doubt. 'Can you, with your telegrams and your newspapers, do better? Always hearing and telling some new thing,' he went on. 'My friend, has your God ever smitten a European nation for gossiping in the bazars? India has gossiped for centuries—always standing in the bazars until the soldiers go by. Therefore—you are here to-day instead of starving in your own country, and I am not a Mohammedan—I am a Product— a Demnition Product. That also I owe to you and yours: that I cannot make an end to my sentence without quoting from your authors.' He pulled at the hookah and mourned, half feelingly, half in earnest, for the shattered hopes of his youth. Wali Dad was always mourning over something or other—the country of which he despaired, or the creed in which he had lost faith, or the life of the English which he could by no means understand.

Lalun never mourned. She played little songs on the sitar, and to hear her sing, 'O Peacock, cry again,' was always a fresh pleasure. She knew all the songs that have ever been sung, from the war-songs of the South, that make the old men angry with the young men and the young men angry with the State, to the love-songs of the North, where the swords whinny-whicker like angry kites in the pauses between the kisses, and the Passes fill with armed men, and the Lover is torn from his Beloved and cries Ai! Ai! Ai! evermore. She knew how to make up tobacco for the pipe so that it smelt like the Gates of Paradise and wafted you gently through them. She could embroider strange things in gold and silver, and dance softly with the moonlight when it came in at the window. Also she knew the hearts of men, and the heart of the City, and whose wives were faithful and whose untrue, and more of the secrets of the Government Offices than are good to be set down in this place. Nasiban, her maid, said that her jewelry was worth ten thousand pounds, and that, some night, a thief would enter and murder her for its possession; but Lalun said that all the City would tear that thief limb from limb, and that he, whoever he was, knew it.

So she took her sitar and sat in the window-seat, and sang a song of old days that had been sung by a girl of her profession in an armed camp on the eve of a great battle—the day before the Fords of the Jumna ran red and Sivaji fled fifty miles to Delhi with a Toorkh stallion at his horse's tail and another Lalun on his saddle-bow. It was what men call a Mahratta laonee, and it said:—

Their warrior forces Chimnajee
    Before the Peishwa led,
The Children of the Sun and Fire
    Behind him turned and fled.

And the chorus said:

With them there fought who rides so free
   With sword and turban red,
The warrior-youth who earns his fee
   At peril of his head.

'At peril of his head,' said Wali Dad in English to me. 'Thanks to your Government, all our heads are protected, and with the educational facilities at my command'—his eyes twinkled wickedly—'I might be a distinguished member of the local administration. Perhaps, in time, I might even be a member of a Legislative Council.'

'Don't speak English,' said Lalun, bending over her sitar afresh. The chorus went out from the City wall to the blackened wall of Fort Amara which dominates the City. No man knows the precise extent of Fort Amara. Three kings built it hundreds of years ago, and they say that there are miles of underground rooms beneath its walls. It is peopled with many ghosts, a detachment of Garrison Artillery, and a Company of Infantry. In its prime it held ten thousand men and filled its ditches with corpses.

'At peril of his head,' sang Lalun again and again.

A head moved on one of the ramparts—the grey head of an old man—and a voice, rough as shark-skin on a sword-hilt, sent back the last line of the chorus and broke into a song that I could not understand, though Lalun and Wali Dad listened intently.

'What is it?' I asked. 'Who is it?'

'A consistent man,' said Wali Dad. 'He fought you in '46, when he was a warrior-youth; refought you in '57, and he tried to fight you in '71, but you had learned the trick of blowing men from guns too well. Now he is old; but he would still fight if he could.'

'Is he a Wahabi, then? Why should he answer to a Mahratta laonee if he be Wahabi—or Sikh?' said I.

'I do not know,' said Wali Dad. 'He has lost, perhaps, his religion. Perhaps he wishes to be a King. Perhaps he is a King. I do not know his name.'

'That is a lie, Wali Dad. If you know his career you must know his name.'

'That is quite true. I belong to a nation of liars. I would rather not tell you his name. Think for yourself.'

Lalun finished her song, pointed to the Fort, and said simply: 'Khem Singh.'

'Hm,' said Wali Dad. 'If the Pearl chooses to tell you, the Pearl is a fool.'

I translated to Lalun, who laughed. 'I choose to tell what I choose to tell. They kept Khem Singh in Burma,' said she. 'They kept him there for many years until his mind was changed in him. So great was the kindness of the Government. Finding this, they sent him back to his own country that he might look upon it before he died. He is an old man, but when he looks upon this his country his memory will come. Moreover, there be many who remember him.'

'He is an Interesting Survival,' said Wali Dad, pulling at the pipe. 'He returns to a country now full of educational and political reform, but, as the Pearl says, there are many who remember him. He was once a great man. There will never be any more great men in India. They will all, when they are boys, go whoring after strange gods, and they will become citizens—"fellow-citizens"—"illustrious fellow-citizens." What is it that the native papers call them?'

Wali Dad seemed to be in a very bad temper. Lalun looked out of the window and smiled into the dust-haze. I went away thinking about Khem Singh, who had once made history with a thousand followers, and would have been a princeling but for the power of the Supreme Government aforesaid.

The Senior Captain Commanding Fort Amara was away on leave, but the Subaltern, his Deputy, had drifted down to the Club, where I found him and inquired of him whether it was really true that a political prisoner had been added to the attractions of the Fort. The Subaltern explained at great length, for this was the first time that he had held command of the Fort, and his glory lay heavy upon him.

'Yes,' said he, 'a man was sent in to me about a week ago from down the line—a thorough gentleman, whoever he is. Of course I did all I could for him. He had his two servants and some silver cooking-pots, and he looked for all the world like a native officer. I called him Subadar Sahib. Just as well to be on the safe side, y'know. "Look here, Subadar Sahib," I said, "you're handed over to my authority, and I'm supposed to guard you. Now I don't want to make your life hard, but you must make things easy for me. All the Fort is at your disposal, from the flagstaff to the dry Ditch, and I shall be happy to entertain you in any way I can, but you mustn't take advantage of it. Give me your word that you won't try to escape, Subadar Sahib, and I'll give you my word that you shall have no heavy guard put over you." I thought the best way of getting at him was by going at him straight, y'know; and it was, by Jove! The old man gave me his word, and moved about the Fort as contented as a sick crow. He's a rummy chap—always asking to be told where he is and what the buildings about him are. I had to sign a slip of blue paper when he turned up, acknowledging receipt of his body and all that, and I'm responsible, y'know, that he doesn't get away. Queer thing, though, looking after a Johnnie old enough to be your grandfather, isn't it? Come to the Fort one of these days and see him.'

For reasons which will appear, I never went to the Fort while Khem Singh was then within its walls. I knew him only as a grey head seen from Lalun's window—a grey head and a harsh voice. But natives told me that, day by day, as he looked upon the fair lands round Amara, his memory came back to him and, with it, the old hatred against the Government that had been nearly effaced in far-off Burma. So he raged up and down the West face of the Fort from morning till noon and from evening till the night, devising vain things in his heart, and croaking war-songs when Lalun sang on the City wall. As he grew more acquainted with the Subaltern he unburdened his old heart of some of the passions that had withered it. 'Sahib,' he used to say, tapping his stick against the parapet, 'when I was a young man I was one of twenty thousand horsemen who came out of the City and rode round the plain here. Sahib, I was the leader of a hundred, then of a thousand, then of five thousand, and now!'—he pointed to his two servants. 'But from the beginning to to-day I would cut the throats of all the Sahibs in the land if I could. Hold me fast, Sahib, lest I get away and return to those who would follow me. I forgot them when I was in Burma, but now that I am in my own country again, I remember everything.'

'Do you remember that you have given me your Honour not to make your tendance a hard matter? ' said the Subaltern.

'Yes, to you, only to you, Sahib,' said Khem Singh. 'To you because you are of a pleasant countenance. If my turn comes again, Sahib, I will not hang you nor cut your throat.'

'Thank you,' said the Subaltern gravely, as he looked along the line of guns that could pound the City to powder in half an hour. 'Let us go into our own quarters, Khem Singh. Come and talk with me after dinner.'

Khem Singh would sit on his own cushion at the Subaltern's feet, drinking heavy, scented aniseed brandy in great gulps, and telling strange stories of Fort Amara, which had been a palace in the old days, of Begums and Ranees tortured to death—in the very vaulted chamber that now served as a mess-room; would tell stories of Sobraon that made the Subaltern's cheeks flush and tingle with pride of race, and of the Kuka rising from which so much was expected and the fore-knowledge of which was shared by a hundred thousand souls. But he never told tales of '57 because, as he said, he was the Subaltern's guest, and '57 is a year that no man, Black or White, cares to speak of. Once only, when the aniseed brandy had slightly affected his head, he said 'Sahib, speaking now of a matter which lay between Sobraon and the affair of the Kukas, it was ever a wonder to us that you stayed your hand at all, and that, having stayed it, you did not make the land one prison. Now I hear from without that you do great honour to all men of our country and by your own hands are destroying the Terror of your Name which is your strong rock and defence. This is a foolish thing. Will oil and water mix? Now in '57—'

'I was not born then, Subadar Sahib,' said the Subaltern, and Khem Singh reeled to his quarters.

The Subaltern would tell me of these conversations at the Club, and my desire to see Khem Singh increased. But Wali Dad, sitting in the windowseat of the house on the City wall, said that it would be a cruel thing to do, and Lalun pretended that I preferred the society of a grizzled old Sikh to hers.

'Here is tobacco, here is talk, here are many friends and all the news of the City, and, above all, here is myself. I will tell you stories and sing you songs, and Wali Dad will talk his English nonsense in your ears. Is that worse than watching the caged animal yonder? Go to-morrow then, if you must, but to-day such-and-such an one will be here, and he will speak of wonderful things.'

It happened that To-morrow never came, and the warm heat of the latter Rains gave place to the chill of early October almost before I was aware of the flight of the year. The Captain Commanding the

Fort returned from leave and took over charge of Khem Singh according to the laws of seniority. The Captain was not a nice man. He called all natives 'niggers,' which, besides being extreme bad form, shows gross ignorance.

'What's the use of telling off two Tommies to watch that old nigger?' said he.

'I fancy it soothes his vanity,' said the Subaltern. 'The men are ordered to keep well out of his way, but he takes them as a tribute to his importance, poor old chap.'

'I won't have Line men taken off regular guards in this way. Put on a couple of Native Infantry.'

'Sikhs?' said the Subaltern, lifting his eyebrows.

'Sikhs, Pathans, Dogras—they're all alike, these black people,' and the Captain talked to Khem Singh in a manner which hurt that old gentleman's feelings. Fifteen years before, when he had been caught for the second time, every one looked upon him as a sort of tiger. He liked being regarded in this light. But he forgot that the world goes forward in fifteen years, and many Subalterns are promoted to Captaincies.

'The Captain-pig is in charge of the Fort?' said Khem Singh to his native guard every morning. And the native guard said: 'Yes, Subadar Sahib,' in deference to his age and his air of distinction; but they did not know who he was.

In those days the gathering in Lalun's little white room was always large and talked more than before.

'The Greeks,' said Wali Dad, who had been borrowing my books, 'the inhabitants of the city of Athens, where they were always hearing and telling some new thing, rigorously secluded their women—who were fools. Hence the glorious institution of the heterodox women—is it not?—who were amusing and not fools. All the Greek philosophers delighted in their company. Tell me, my friend, how it goes now in Greece and the other places upon the Continent of Europe. Are your women-folk also fools?'

'Wali Dad,' I said, 'you never speak to us about your women-folk and we never speak about ours to you. That is the bar between us.'

'Yes,' said Wali Dad, 'it is curious to think that our common meeting-place should be here, in the house of a common—how do you call her?' He pointed with the pipe-mouth to Lalun.

'Lalun is nothing but Lalun,' I said, and that was perfectly true. 'But if you took your place in the world, Wali Dad, and gave up dreaming dreams—'

'I might wear an English coat and trousers. I might be a leading Mohammedan pleader. I might be received even at the Commissioner's tennis-parties where the English stand on one side and the natives on the other, in order to promote social intercourse throughout the Empire. Heart's Heart,' said he to Lalun quickly, 'the Sahib says that I ought to quit you.'

'The Sahib is always talking stupid talk,' returned Lalun with a laugh. 'In this house I am a Queen and thou art a King. The Sahib' she put her arms above her head and thought for a moment—'the Sahib shall be our Vizier—thine and mine, Wali Dad—because he has said that thou shouldst leave me.'

Wali Dad laughed immoderately, and I laughed too. 'Be it so,' said he. 'My friend, are you willing to take this lucrative Government appointment? Lalun, what shall his pay be?'

But Lalun began to sing, and for the rest of the time there was no hope of getting a sensible answer from her or Wali Dad. When the one stopped, the other began to quote Persian poetry with a triple pun in every other line. Some of it was not strictly proper, but it was all very funny, and it only came to an end when a fat person in black, with gold pince-nez, sent up his name to Lalun, and Wali Dad dragged me into the twinkling night to walk in a big rose-garden and talk heresies about Religion and Governments and a man's career in life.

The Mohurrum, the great mourning-festival of the Mohammedans, was close at hand, and the things that Wali Dad said about religious fanaticism would have secured his expulsion from the loosest-thinking Muslim sect. There were the rose-bushes round us, the stars above us, and from every quarter of the City came the boom of the big Mohurrum drums. You must know that the City is divided in fairly equal proportions between the Hindus and the Mussulmans, and where both creeds belong to the fighting races, a big religious festival gives ample chance for trouble. When they can—that is to say, when the authorities are weak enough to allow it—the Hindus do their best to arrange some minor feast-day of their own in time to clash with the period of general mourning for the martyrs Hasan and Hussain, the heroes of the Mohurrum. Gilt and painted paper representations of their tombs are borne with shouting and wailing, music, torches, and yells, through the principal thoroughfares of the City; which fakements are called tazias. Their passage is rigorously laid down beforehand by the Police, and detachments of Police accompany each tazia, lest the Hindus should throw bricks at it and the peace of the Queen and the heads of Her loyal subjects should thereby be broken. Mohurrum time in a 'fighting' town means anxiety to all the officials, because, if a riot breaks out, the officials and not the rioters are held responsible. The former must foresee everything, and while not making their precautions ridiculously elaborate, must see that they are at least adequate.

'Listen to the drums!' said Wali Dad. 'That is the heart of the people—empty and making much noise. How, think you, will the Mohurrum go this year? I think that there will be trouble.'

He turned down a side-street and left me alone with the stars and a sleepy Police patrol. Then I went to bed and dreamed that Wali Dad had sacked the City and I was made Vizier, with Lalun's silver pipe for mark of office.

All day the Mohurrum drums beat in the City, and all day deputations of tearful Hindu gentlemen besieged the Deputy-Commissioner with assurances that they would be murdered ere next dawning by the Mohammedans. 'Which,' said the Deputy-Commissioner, in confidence to the Head of Police, 'is a pretty fair indication that the Hindus are going to make 'emselves unpleasant. I think we can arrange a little surprise for them. I have given the heads of both Creeds fair warning. If they choose to disregard it, so much the worse for them.'

There was a large gathering in Lalun's house that night, but of men that I had never seen before, if I except the fat gentleman in black with the gold pince-nez. Wali Dad lay in the window-seat, more bitterly scornful of his Faith and its manifestations than I had ever known him. Lalun's maid was very busy cutting up and mixing tobacco for the guests. We could hear the thunder of the drums as the processions accompanying each tazia marched to the central gathering-place in the plain outside the City, preparatory to their triumphant re-entry and circuit within the walls. All the streets seemed ablaze with torches, and only Fort Amara was black and silent.

When the noise of the drums ceased, no one in the white room spoke for a time. 'The first tazia has moved off,' said Wali Dad, looking to the plain.

'That is very early,' said the man with the pince-nez. 'It is only half-past eight.' The company rose and departed.

'Some of them were men from Ladakh,' said Lalun, when the last had gone. 'They brought me brick-tea such as the Russians sell, and a tea-urn from Peshawur. Show me, now, how the English Memsahibs make tea.'

The brick-tea was abominable. When it was finished Wali Dad suggested going into the streets. 'I am nearly sure that there will be trouble to-night,' he said. 'All the City thinks so, and Vox Populi is Vox Dei, as the Babus say. Now I tell you that at the corner of the Padshahi Gate you will find my horse all this night if you want to go about and to see things. It is a most disgraceful exhibition. Where is the pleasure of saying "Ya Hasan! a Hussain!" twenty thousand times in a night?'

All the processions—there were two-and-twenty of them—were now well within the City walls. The drums were beating afresh, the crowd were howling 'Ya Hasan! a Hussain!' and beating their breasts, the brass bands were playing their loudest, and at every corner where space allowed, Mohammedan preachers were telling the lamentable story of the death of the Martyrs. It was impossible to move except with the crowd, for the streets were not more than twenty feet wide. In the Hindu quarters the shutters of all the shops were up and cross-barred. As the first tazia, a gorgeous erection, ten feet high, was borne aloft on the shoulders of a score of stout men into the semi-darkness of the Gully of the Horsemen, a brickbat crashed through its talc and tinsel sides.

'Into thy hands, O Lord!' murmured Wali Dad profanely, as a yell went up from behind, and a native officer of Police jammed his horse through the crowd. Another brickbat followed, and the tazia staggered and swayed where it had stopped.

'Go on! In the name of the Sirkar, go forward!' shouted the Policeman, but there was an ugly cracking and splintering of shutters, and the crowd halted, with oaths and growlings, before the house whence the brickbat had been thrown.

Then, without any warning, broke the storm—not only in the Gully of the Horsemen, but in half-a-dozen other places. The tazias rocked like ships at sea, the long pole-torches dipped and rose round them while the men shouted: 'The Hindus are dishonouring the tazias! Strike! strike! Into their temples for the Faith!' The six or eight Policemen with each tazia drew their batons, and struck as long as they could in the hope of forcing the mob forward, but they were overpowered, and as contingents of Hindus poured into the streets, the fight became general. Half a mile away where the tazias were yet untouched the drums and the shrieks of 'Ya Hasan! Ya Hussain!' continued, but not for long. The priests at the corners of the streets knocked the legs from the bedsteads that supported their pulpits and smote for the Faith, while stones fell from the silent houses upon friend and foe, and the packed streets bellowed: 'Din! Din! Din!' A tazia caught fire, and was dropped for a flaming barrier between Hindu and Mussulman at the corner of the Gully. Then the crowd surged forward, and Wali Dad drew me close to the stone pillar of a well.

'It was intended from the beginning!' he shouted in my ear, with more heat than blank unbelief should be guilty of. 'The bricks were carried up to the houses beforehand. These swine of Hindus! We shall be killing kine in their temples to-night!'

Tazia after tazia, some burning, others torn to pieces, hurried past us and the mob with them, howling, shrieking, and striking at the house doors in their flight. At last we saw the reason of the rush. Hugonin, the Assistant District Superintendent of Police, a boy of twenty, had got together thirty constables and was forcing the crowd through the streets. His old grey Policehorse showed no sign of uneasiness as it was spurred breast—on into the crowd, and the long dog-whip with which he had armed himself was never still.

'They know we haven't enough Police to hold 'em,' he cried as he passed me, mopping a cut on his face. 'They know we haven't! Aren't any of the men from the Club coming down to help? Get on, you sons of burnt fathers!' The dog-whip cracked across the writhing backs, and the constables smote afresh with baton and gun-butt. With these passed the lights and the shouting, and Wali Dad began to swear under his breath. From Fort Amara shot up a single rocket; then two side by side. It was the signal for troops.

Petitt, the Deputy-Commissioner, covered with dust and sweat, but calm and gently smiling, cantered up the clean-swept street in rear of the main body of the rioters. 'No one killed yet,' he shouted. 'I'll keep 'em on the run till dawn! Don't let 'em halt, Hugonin! Trot 'em about till the troops come.'

The science of the defence lay solely in keeping the mob on the move. If they had breathing-space they would halt and fire a house, and then the work of restoring order would be more difficult, to say the least of it. Flames have the same effect on a crowd as blood has on a wild beast.

Word had reached the Club, and men in evening-dress were beginning to show themselves and lend a hand in heading off and breaking up the shouting masses with stirrup-leathers, whips, or chance-found staves. They were not very often attacked, for the rioters had sense enough to know that the death of a European would not mean one hanging but many, and possibly the appearance of the thrice-dreaded Artillery. The clamour in the City redoubled. The Hindus had descended into the streets in real earnest and ere long the mob returned. It was a strange sight. There were no tazias—only their riven platforms—and there were no Police. Here and there a City dignitary, Hindu or Mohammedan, was vainly imploring his co-religionists to keep quiet and behave themselves—advice for which his white beard was pulled. Then a native officer of Police, unhorsed but still using his spurs with effect, would be borne along, warning all the crowd of the danger of insulting the Government. Everywhere men struck aimlessly with sticks, grasping each other by the throat, howling and foaming with rage, or beat with their bare hands on the doors of the houses.

'It is a lucky thing that they are fighting with natural weapons,' I said to Wali Dad, 'else we should have half the City killed.'

I turned as I spoke and looked at his face. His nostrils were distended, his eyes were fixed, and he was smiting himself softly on the breast. The crowd poured by with renewed riot—a gang of Mussulmans hard pressed by some hundred Hindu fanatics. Wali Dad left my side with an oath, and shouting: 'Ya Hasan! Ya Hussain!' plunged into the thick of the fight, where I lost sight of him.

I fled by a side alley to the Padshahi Gate, where I found Wali Dad's horse, and thence rode to the Fort. Once outside the City wall, the tumult sank to a dull roar, very impressive under the stars and reflecting great credit on the fifty thousand angry able-bodied men who were making it. The troops who, at the Deputy-Commissioner's instance, had been ordered to rendezvous quietly near the Fort, showed no signs of being impressed. Two companies of Native Infantry, a squadron of Native Cavalry, and a company of British Infantry were kicking their heels in the shadow of the East face, waiting for orders to march in. I am sorry to say that they were all pleased, unholily pleased, at the chance of what they called 'a little fun.' The senior officers, to be sure, grumbled at having been kept out of bed, and the English troops pretended to be sulky, but there was joy in the hearts of all the subalterns, and whispers ran up and down the line: 'No ball-cartridge—what a beastly shame!' 'D'you think the beggars will really stand up to us?' 'Hope I shall meet my money-lender there. I owe him more than I can afford.' 'Oh, they won't let us even unsheath swords.' 'Hurrah! Up goes the fourth rocket. Fall in, there!'

The Garrison Artillery, who to the last cherished a wild hope that they might be allowed to bombard the City at a hundred yards' range, lined the parapet above the East gateway and cheered themselves hoarse as the British Infantry doubled along the road to the Main Gate of the City. The Cavalry cantered on to the Padshahi Gate, and the Native Infantry marched slowly to the Gate of the Butchers. The surprise was intended to be of a distinctly unpleasant nature, and to come on top of the defeat of the Police, who had been just able to keep the Mohammedans from firing the houses of a few leading Hindus. The bulk of the riot lay in the north and north-west wards. The east and south-east were by this time dark and silent, and I rode hastily to Lalun's house, for I wished to tell her to send some one in search of Wali Dad. The house was unlighted, but the door was open, and I climbed upstairs in the darkness. One small lamp in the white room showed Lalun and her maid leaning half out of the window, breathing heavily and evidently pulling at something that refused to come.

'Thou art late—very late,' gasped Lalun without turning her head. 'Help us now, O Fool, if thou hast not spent thy strength howling among the tazias. Pull! Nasiban and I can do no more! O Sahib, is it you? The Hindus have been hunting an old Mohammedan round the Ditch with clubs. If they find him again they will kill him. Help us to pull him up.'

I put my hands to the long red silk waist-cloth that was hanging out of the window, and we three pulled and pulled with all the strength at our command. There was something very heavy at the end, and it swore in an unknown tongue as it kicked against the City wall.

'Pull, oh, pull!' said Lalun at the last. A pair of brown hands grasped the window-sill and a venerable Mohammedan tumbled upon the floor, very much out of breath. His jaws were tied up, his turban had fallen over one eye, and he was dusty and angry.

Lalun hid her face in her hands for an instant and said something about Wali Dad that I could not catch.

Then, to my extreme gratification, she threw her arms round my neck and murmured pretty things. I was in no haste to stop her; and Nasiban, being a handmaiden of tact, turned to the big jewel-chest that stands in the corner of the white room and rummaged among the contents. The Mohammedan sat on the floor and glared.

'One service more, Sahib, since thou hast come so opportunely,' said Lalun. 'Wilt thou'—it is very nice to be thou-ed by Lalun—'take this old man across the City—the troops are everywhere, and they might hurt him, for he is old—to the Kumharsen Gate? There I think he may find a carriage to take him to his house. He is a friend of mine, and thou art—more than a friend—therefore I ask this.'

Nasiban bent over the old man, tucked something into his belt, and I raised him up and led him into the streets. In crossing from the east to the west of the City there was no chance of avoiding the troops and the crowd. Long before I reached the Gully of the Horsemen I heard the shouts of the British Infantry crying cheerily 'Hutt, ye beggars! Hutt, ye devils! Get along Go forward, there!' Then followed the ringing of rifle-butts and shrieks of pain. The troops were banging the bare toes of the mob with their gun-butts—for not a bayonet had been fixed. My companion mumbled and jabbered as we walked on until we were carried back by the crowd and had to force our way to the troops. I caught him by the wrist and felt a bangle there—the iron bangle of the Sikhs—but I had no suspicions, for Lalun had only ten minutes before put her arms round me. Thrice we were carried back by the crowd, and when we made our way past the British Infantry it was to meet the Sikh Cavalry driving another mob before them with the butts of their lances.

'What are these dogs?' said the old man.

'Sikhs of the Cavalry, Father,' I said, and we edged our way up the line of horses two abreast and found the Deputy-Commissioner, his helmet smashed on his head, surrounded by a knot of men who had come down from the Club as amateur constables and had helped the Police mightily.

'We'll keep 'em on the run till dawn,' said Petitt. 'Who's your villainous friend? '

I had only time to say: 'The Protection of the Sirkar!' when a fresh crowd flying before the Native Infantry carried us a hundred yards nearer to the Kumharsen Gate, and Petitt was swept away like a shadow.

'I do not know—I cannot see—this is all new to me!' moaned my companion. 'How many troops are there in the City?'

'Perhaps five hundred,' I said.

'A lakh of men beaten by five hundred—and Sikhs among them! Surely, surely, I am an old man, but—the Kumharsen Gate is new. Who pulled down the stone lions? Where is the conduit? Sahib, I am a very old man, and, alas, I—I cannot stand.' He dropped in the shadow of the Kumharsen Gate where there was no disturbance. A fat gentleman wearing gold pince-nez came out of the darkness.

'You are most kind to bring my old friend,' he said suavely. 'He is a landholder of Akala. He should not be in a big City when there is religious excitement. But I have a carriage here. You are quite truly kind. Will you help me to put him into the carriage? It is very late.'

We bundled the old man into a hired victoria that stood close to the gate, and I turned back to the house on the City wall. The troops were driving the people to and fro, while the Police shouted, 'To your houses! Get to your houses!' and the dog-whip of the Assistant District Superintendent cracked remorselessly. Terror-stricken bunnias clung to the stirrups of the Cavalry, crying that their houses had been robbed (which was a lie), and the burly Sikh horsemen patted them on the shoulder and bade them return to those houses lest a worse thing should happen. Parties of five or six British soldiers, joining arms, swept down the side-gullies, their rifles on their backs, stamping, with shouting and song, upon the toes of Hindu and Mussulman. Never was religious enthusiasm more systematically squashed; and never were poor breakers of the peace more utterly weary and footsore. They were routed out of holes and corners, from behind well-pillars and byres, and bidden to go to their houses. If they had no houses to go to, so much the worse for their toes.

On returning to Lalun's door I stumbled over a man at the threshold. He was sobbing hysterically and his arms flapped like the wings of a goose. It was Wali Dad, Agnostic and Unbeliever, shoeless, turbanless, and frothing at the mouth, the flesh on his chest bruised and bleeding from the vehemence with which he had smitten himself. A broken torch-handle lay by his side, and his quivering lips murmured, 'Ya Hasan! Ya Hussain!' as I stooped over him. I pushed him a few steps up the staircase, threw a pebble at Lalun's City window and hurried home.

Most of the streets were very still, and the cold wind that comes before the dawn whistled down them. In the centre of the Square of the Mosque a man was bending over a corpse. The skull had been smashed in by gun-butt or bamboo-stave.

'It is expedient that one man should die for the people,' said Petitt grimly, raising the shape less head. 'These brutes were beginning to show their teeth too much.'

And from afar we could hear the soldiers singing 'Two Lovely Black Eyes' as they drove the remnant of the rioters within doors.

Of course you can guess what happened? I was not so clever. When the news went abroad that Khem Singh had escaped from the Fort, I did not, since I was then living this story, not writing it, connect myself, or Lalun, or the fat gentleman of the gold pince-nez, with his disappearance. Nor did it strike me that Wali Dad was the man who should have convoyed him across the City, or that Lalun's arms round my neck were put there to hide the money that Nasiban gave to Khem Singh, and that Lalun had used me and my white face as even a better safeguard than Wali Dad who proved himself so untrustworthy. All that I knew at the time was that, when Fort Amara was taken up with the riots, Khem Singh profited by the confusion to get away, and that his two Sikh guards also escaped.

But later on I received full enlightenment; and so did Khem Singh. He fled to those who knew him in the old days, but many of them were dead and more were changed, and all knew something of the Wrath of the Government. He went to the young men, but the glamour of his name had passed away, and they were entering native regiments or Government offices, and Khem Singh could give them neither pension, decorations, nor influence—nothing but a glorious death with their back to the mouth of a gun. He wrote letters and made promises, and the letters fell into bad hands, and a wholly insignificant subordinate officer of Police tracked them down and gained promotion thereby. Moreover, Khem Singh was old, and aniseed brandy was scarce, and he had left his silver cooking-pots in Fort Amara with his nice warm bedding, and the gentleman with the gold pince-nez was told by Those who had employed him that Khem Singh as a popular leader was not worth the money paid.

'Great is the mercy of these fools of English!' said Khem Singh when the situation was put before him. 'I will go back to Fort Amara of my own free will and gain honour. Give me good clothes to return in.'

So, at his own time, Khem Singh knocked at the wicket-gate of the Fort and walked to the Captain and the Subaltern, who were nearly grey-headed on account of correspondence that daily arrived from Simla marked 'Private.'

'I have come back, Captain Sahib,' said Khem Singh. 'Put no more guards over me. It is no good out yonder.'

A week later I saw him for the first time to my knowledge, and he made as though there were an understanding between us.

'It was well done, Sahib,' said he, 'and greatly I admired your astuteness in thus boldly facing the troops when I, whom they would have doubtless torn to pieces, was with you. Now there is a man in Fort Ooltagarh whom a bold man could with ease help to escape. This is the position of the Fort as I draw it on the sand—'

But I was thinking how I had become Lalun's Vizier after all.

Rudyard Kipling – A Short Biography

Born in Bombay on 30th December 1865, Joseph Rudyard Kipling wrote short stories, poems and novels, a body of work whose reputation is in constant flux as his presentations and interpretations of empire are viewed within the changing context of empirical absolution in the twentieth century. Having spent the first five years of his life in India he felt a natural affinity for the country, though his upbringing had a distinctly colonial taste flavour. He was born in the Bombay Presidency of British India to Lockwood Kipling, an English art teacher and illustrator who took a position as professor of architectural sculpture in the Jeejeebhoy School of Art and Alice MacDonald, spoken of by the a Viceroy of India that "dullness and Mrs Kipling cannot exist in the same room". Though their presence in India was principally artistic and educational, rather than political, the company they kept and the establishments in which they kept it indicate an existence very much benefitting from the British Empire. Lockwood would later go on to assume a position as curator of the Lahore Museum, while working on various illustrations for Rudyard's writing, and various decorations for the Victoria and Albert museum in London. Much of his work, then, was coloured by the empire, whether in service to or benefitting from, and it was into this distinctly British experience of India that Rudyard was born.

Lockwood and Alice had met and fallen in love at Rudyard Lake in Rudyard, Staffordshire, and their affections for the area were so great they chose to refer to the lake in naming their first-born. Alice came from a family of four sisters, all of whose marriages were significant and well-arranged; moreover, Rudyard's most famous relative was Stanley Baldwin, Conservative Prime Minister on three occasions in the 1920s and 1930s. Kipling's sense of belonging in Bombay is found in 'To the City of Bombay' in the dedication to Seven Seas, a collection of poems published in 1900, which reads:—

> Mother of Cities to me,
> For I was born in her gate,
> Between the palms and the sea,
> Where the world-end steamers
> wait.

His parents considered themselves Anglo-Indians, and he would later assume this classification although he did not live there long. His first five years, which he describes as days of "strong light and darkness", ended when he and his three-year-old sister Alice were removed to Southsea, Plymouth, to board with Captain Pryse Agar Holloway and his wife Mrs Sarah Holloway, a couple who cared for the children of couples born in British India. They were there for six years and Kipling would later recall their time there with horror, describing incidents of cruelty and neglect and wondering whether it was these which speeded up his literary maturity, for "it made me give attention to the lies I soon found it necessary to tell: and this, I presume, is the foundation of literary effort".

Alice's time, by contrast, was relatively comfortable, Mrs Holloway hoping that she would marry her son, though this ambition would not come to fruition. They did have relatives in England, a maternal aunt Georgiana and her husband who lived in Fulham, London, in a house at which they spent a month each Christmas and which Kipling later described as "a paradise which I verily believe saved me". Their mother returned in 1877 and removed them from their custody with the Holloways. A year later he gained admission to the United Services College at Westward Ho! in Devon, a recently established school with the intention of readying boys for military service in the British Army. His time here was fraught physically, though emotionally it proved fruitful for he began several firm friendships with other boys at the school. Moreover, he found in it inspiration for the setting of his series of schoolboy stories, Stalky and Co, begun in 1899. Meanwhile, his sister Alice had returned to Southsea and was boarding with Florence Garrard, with whom he fell in love and on whom he modeled Maisie in his first novel, The Light That Failed, published in 1891. At sixteen he was found lacking in the academic perspicacity necessary to undertake a scholarship to Oxford University, his parents meanwhile lacking the wherewithal to finance him therein. As such his father sought a job for him in Lahore, Punjab, where he was now a museum curator. The position he found for his son was as assistant editor of the Civil and Military Gazette, a small local newspaper. Kipling left for India on 20th September 1882, arriving in Bombay on 18th October. "There were yet three or four days" rail to Lahore, where my people lived. After these, my English years fell away, nor ever, I think, came back in full strength".

The Gazette appeared six days of the week, year-round save for a short break at both Christmas and Easter. Its editor Stephen Wheeler was diligent but Kipling's writing was insatiable, and he came to consider the paper his "mistress and most true love". In the summer of 1883 Kipling visited Shimla, the colonial hill-station and summer capital of British India which was then called Simla.

Chosen by the British owing to its resemblance of English climate and scenery (as far as was possible in India), it became the seat of the Viceroy of India for the six months on the plains which were too hot for the British temperament, and subsequently became a "centre of power as well as pleasure". Lockwood was asked to serve in the Church there, and his family became yearly visitors while Kipling himself would take his annual leave here from 1885-88. The value of this time is evident from the regularity with which Simla appears in his writing for the Gazette, which in his journals he describes the time as

> "….pure joy—every golden hour counted. It began in heat and discomfort, by rail and road. It ended in the cool evening, with a wood fire in one's bedroom, and next morn—thirty more of them ahead!—the early cup of tea, the Mother who brought it in, and the long talks of us all together again."

In 1886, his Departmental Ditties appeared, his first collection of verse, and brought with it a change of editor; Kay Robinson, Wheeler's replacement, was in favour of Kipling's creativity and granted him more freedom in that respect, even asking him to write short stories to appear in the newspaper. The vivacity of his writing was captured in a description of him by an ex-colleague at the Gazette, saying he "never knew such a fellow for ink—he simply revelled in it, filling up his pen viciously, and then throwing the contents all over the office, so that it was almost dangerous to approach him". While in Lahore, he had thirty-nine stories published in the Gazette between November 1886 and June 1887. Most of these are compiled in Plain Tales from the Hills, his first collection of prose, which was published in January 1888 in Calcutta, shortly after his 22nd birthday. In November 1887, he transferred from the Gazette to its much larger sister newspaper, The Pioneer, based in Allahabad. The pace of his writing remained, and in 1888 he published six collections of stories, Soldiers Three,

The Story of the Gadsbys, In Black and White, Under the Deodars, The Phantom Rickshaw and Wee Willie Winkie, composed of some 41 stories. In addition, his position as The Pioneer's special correspondent in the Western region of Rajputna, he wrote many sketches which were later compiled in Letters of Marque and published in From Sea to Sea and Other Sketches, Letters of Travel.

A dispute in 1889 saw him discharged from The Pioneer, though by now he had been considering his future and sold the rights to his six volumes of stories for £200 and a small royalty, while the Plain Tales fetched £50, along with six months' salary from The Pioneer in lieu of notice. Using the money to undertake a pilgrimage to London, the literary centre of the British Empire, he left India on 9th March 1889, travelling via Rangoon, San Francisco, Hong Kong and Japan, then through the United States writing articles for The Pioneer which were also included in From Sea to Sea and Other Sketches, Letters of Travel. Arriving in England at Liverpool on October 1889, London and his literary début there beckoned.

His first task was to find a place to live, and he eventually settled on quarters in Villiers Street, Strand. The next two years saw several stories accepted by various magazine editors, the publication of the novel The Light That Failed, a nervous breakdown, the collaboration with Wolcott Balestier on the novel (uncharacterstically misspelt) The Naulhaka, and in 1891, following his doctors' advice, he embarked on a further sea voyage, travelling to South Africa, Australia, New Zealand and also returning to India. His plans to spend Christmas with his family were cut short on the news of Balestier's sudden death from typhoid fever, prompting an immediate return to London. Before he left, he had proposed to Balestier's sister Caroline Starr Balestier, with whom he had been having a hushed romance for just over a year. Back in London, Life's Handicap was published in 1891, a collection of short stories whose subject was the British in India, and British India. On 18th January 1892 aged 26 he married Caroline in the midst of an epidemic of influenza. Caroline was given away by Henry James, the famous and celebrated American author.

Honeymooning in Japan, they travelled via Vermont, America, to visit the Balestier estate, and upon arrival in Yokahama they found that their bank, The New Oriental Banking Corporation, had failed, though this loss did not deter them and they returned to Vermont, Caroline now pregnant with their first child. Renting a cottage on a farm for $10 per month, they lived a spartan existence and were "extraordinarily and self-centredly content". The named the residence Bliss Cottage, and it was here that the child was born, named Josephine, "in three foot of snow on the night of 29th December 1892. Her Mother's birthday being the 31st and mine the 30th we congratulated her on her sense of the fitness of things." While here, Kipling had his first ideas for the Jungle Books. Shortly after Josephine was born the couple moved in pursuit of more space and comfort, buying ten acres overlooking the Connecticut River from Caroline's brother. The house they built there was inspired by the Mughul architecture he encountered in Lahore, and was named Naulakha (this time correctly spelt) in honour of Wolcott. His literary output in four years here included the Jungle Books, a collection of short stories entitled The Day's Work, the novel Captain Courageous and a plethora of poetry, of which most notably the volume The Seven Seas and his Barrack-Room Ballads. Meanwhile, he enjoyed correspondence with the many children who wrote to him about the Jungle Books.

In between this writing, Kipling took regular visitors. Most notably Arthur Conan Doyle came, bringing golf clubs and staying for two days to give Kipling an extended golf lesson. Kipling enjoyed the game so much that he continued to play, even in winter with special red balls, though he found that the ice would lead to drives travelling two miles as they slid "down the long slope to the Connecticut River". Elsie, the couple's second daughter, was born in February 1896, and by this time it is thought that their marriage had lost its original spark of spontaneity and descended into routine, though they remained loyal to one another. By now, failed arbitration between the United States and England over a border dispute involving British Guiana incited Anglo-American tensions which, in May 1896, resulted in a confrontation between Kipling and Caroline's brother, resulting in his arrest and, in the hearing which followed, the destruction of Kipling's private life, leaving him exhausted and miserable and leading to their return to England.

They had settled Torquay, Devon, by September 1896, and he remained socially present and literarily productive. The success of his writing had brought him fame, and he had responded with a sense of duty to include in his writing elements of political persuasion, most notably in his two poems Recessional and The White Man's Burden, which caused controversy when they were published in 1897 and 1899 respectively. Many considered them anthemic to the empire, propaganda for the imperial mindset so prevalent in the Victoria era. Their first son, John, was born in August 1887. Another journey to South Africa began a tradition of wintering there, which continued until 1908. His reputation as Poet of the Empire saw him well-received by politicians in the Cape Colony, and he started the newspaper The Friend for Lord Roberts and the British troops in Bloemfontein. Back in England, they moved to Rottingdean, East Sussex, in 1897, and in 1902 he bought Bateman's, a house built in 1630, which was his home from until his death in 1936. Kim was published in 1902, after which he collected material for Just So Stories for Little Children, published a year later. Both he and Josephine developed pneumonia while visiting the United States, from which she later died.

This decade proved his most successful, being awarded the Nobel Prize for Literature in 1907, the prize citation reading "in consideration of the power of observation, originality of imagination, virility of ideas and remarkable talent for narration which characterise the creations of this world-famous author". He was the first English-language recipient. At the award ceremony in

Switzerland, Carl David af Wirsén praised Kipling and the English literary tradition:

> The Swedish Academy, in awarding the Nobel Prize in Literature this year to Rudyard Kipling, desires to pay a tribute to the literature of England, so rich in manifold glories, and to the greatest genius in the realm of narrative that that country has produced in our times.

Following this achievement, Kipling published Rewards and Fairies, which contained If, voted Britain's favourite poem in a BBC opinion poll in 1995. He turned down several recommendations for knighthood and was considered for Poet Laureate, though this position was never offered to him.

The sense of perseverance, honour and stoicism in If prevailed in many of his opinions, including that on the First World War. Writing in The New Army in Training in 1915, he scorned those who refused conscription, considering

> ....what will be the position in years to come of the young man who has deliberately elected to outcaste himself from this all-embracing brotherhood? What of his family, and, above all, what of his descendants, when the books have been closed and the last balance struck of sacrifice and sorrow in every hamlet, village, parish, suburb, city, shire, district, province, and Dominion throughout the Empire?

This attitude saw him encourage his son, John, to go to war, and he was promptly killed at the Battle of Loos in September 1915, aged 18. Last seen during the battle stumbling blindly through the mud, screaming in agony after an exploding shell had ripped his face apart, Kipling would write—

"If any question why we died
Tell them, because our fathers lied"

—perhaps betraying the guilt he felt at encouraging his son to go to war and finding him a position in the Irish Guards through his friendship with commander-in-chief Lord Roberts, for whom he had established The Friend in Bloemfontein. His death inspired much of Kipling's successive writing, notably My Boy Jack and a two-volume history of the Irish Guards, considered one of the finest examples of regimental history. Ironically, though his writing and his political position had arguably cost John his life, after the war he became friends with a French soldier whose copy of Kim, kept in his breast pocket, had stopped a bullet and saved his life. For a while the book and the soldier's Croix de Guerre were with Kipling, presented as tokens of gratitude, and they remained in contact, though when Kipling learned of the soldier's child he insisted on returning both book and medal.

He kept writing until 1930, though at a considerably slower pace, and to less success. His death, already once incorrectly announced early by a magazine in a premature obituary (and to which he responded "I've just read that I am dead. Don't forget to delete me from your list of subscribers") came on 18th January 1936, at the age of 70, from a perforated duodenal ulcer. His coffin was carried by, among others, his cousin the Prime Minister Stanley Baldwin, and his marble casket covered by a Union flag. He was cremated at Golders Green Crematorium in Northwest London and his ashes are buried at Poets' Corner in Westminster Abbey, alongside the graves of both Charles Dickens and Thomas Hardy.

In conjunction with various earthly memorials which commemorate him, alongside his extensive writing, he has a crater on Mercury named after him. The question of memorial and monument is much-addressed in English Literature and, as various great authors and poets have agreed before Kipling's time, his memory lives on more vivaciously set in his words, far longer and better represented than it could set in stone.

Rudyard Kipling - A Concise Bibliography

Books
The City of Dreadful Night (1885, short story)
Plain Tales from the Hills (1888)
Soldiers Three (1888)
The Story of the Gadsbys (1888)
In Black and White (1888)
Under the Deodars (1888)
The Phantom 'Rickshaw and other Eerie Tales (1888)
Wee Willie Winkie and Other Child Stories (1888)
Life's Handicap (1891)
The Light that Failed (1891) (novel)
American Notes (1891) (non-fiction)
The Naulahka: A Story of West and East (1892) (with Wolcott Balestie)
Many Inventions (1893)
The Jungle Book (1894)
Mowgli's Brothers (short story)
Kaa's Hunting (short story)
Tiger! Tiger! (short story)
The White Seal (short story)
Rikki-Tikki-Tavi (short story)
Toomai of the Elephants (short story)
Her Majesty's Servants (originally titled Servants of the Queen) (short story)
The Second Jungle Book (1895)
How Fear Came (short story)
The Miracle of Purun Bhagat (short story)
Letting in the Jungle (short story)
The Undertakers (short story)

The King's Ankus (short story)
Quiquern (short story)
Red Dog" (short story)
The Spring Running (short story)
Captains Courageous (1896) (novel)
The Day's Work (1898)
A Fleet in Being (1898)
Stalky & Co. (1899)
From Sea to Sea and Other Sketches, Letters of Travel (1899) (non-fiction)
Kim (1901) (novel)
Just So Stories for Little Children (1902)
Traffics and Discoveries (1904) (24 collected short stories)
With the Night Mail (1905) A Story of 2000 A.D
Puck of Pook's Hill (1906)
The Brushwood Boy (1907)
Actions and Reactions (1909)
A Song of the English (1909) (with W. Heath Robinson illustrator)
Rewards and Fairies (1910)
A History of England (1911) (non-fiction with Charles Robert Leslie Fletcher)
Songs from Books (1912)
As Easy as A.B.C. (1912) (Science-fiction short story)
The Fringes of the Fleet (1915) (non-fiction)
Sea Warfare (1916) (non-fiction)
A Diversity of Creatures (1917)
Land and Sea Tales for Scouts and Guides (1923)
The Irish Guards in the Great War (1923) (non-fiction)
Debits and Credits (1926)
A Book of Words (1928) (non-fiction)
Thy Servant a Dog (1930)
Limits and Renewals (1932)
Tales of India: the Windermere Series (1935)
Something of Myself (1937) (autobiography)
The Elephant's Child (fiction)

A Book of Words (1928)
Something of Myself (1937)

Short Story Collections

Quartette (1885) – with his father, mother, and sister
Plain Tales from the Hills (1888)
Soldiers Three, The Story of the Gadsbys, In Black and White (1888)
The Phantom 'Rickshaw and other Eerie Tales (1888)
Under the Deodars (1888)
Wee Willie Winkie and Other Child Stories (1888)
Life's Handicap (1891)
Many Inventions (1893)
The Jungle Book (1894)
The Second Jungle Book (1895)
The Day's Work (1898)
Life's Handicap (1899)
Stalky & Co. (1899)
Just So Stories (1902)
Traffics and Discoveries (1904)
Puck of Pook's Hill (1906)
Actions and Reactions (1909)
Abaft the Funnel (1909)
Rewards and Fairies (1910)
The Eyes of Asia (1917)
A Diversity of Creatures (1917)
Land and Sea Tales for Scouts and Guides (1923)
Debits and Credits (1926)
Thy Servant a Dog (1930)
Limits and Renewals (1932)

Military Collections

A Fleet in Being (1898)

France at War (1915)
The New Army in Training (1915)
Sea Warfare (1916)
The War in the Mountains (1917)
The Graves of the Fallen (1919)
The Irish Guards in the Great War (1923)

Poetry Collections
Schoolboy Lyrics (1881)
Echoes (1884) – with his sister, Alice ('Trix')
Departmental Ditties (1886)
Barrack-Room Ballads (1890)
The Seven Seas (1896)
An Almanac of Twelve Sports (1898, with illustrations by William Nicholson)
The Five Nations (1903)
Collected Verse (1907)
Songs from Books (1912)
The Years Between (1919)
Rudyard Kipling's Verse: Definitive Edition (1940)
The Muse Among the Motors (poetry)

Travel Writing
From Sea to Sea – Letters of Travel: 1887–1889 (1899)
Letters of Travel: 1892–1913 (1920)
Souvenirs of France (1933)
Brazilian Sketches: 1927 (1940)

Collected Works
The Outward Bound Edition (1897–1937, 36 volumes)
The Edition de Luxe (1897–1937, 38 volumes)
The Bombay Edition (1913–38, 31 volumes)
The Sussex Edition (1937–39, 35 volumes)

The Burwash Edition (1941, 28 volumes)

Poems
Departmental Ditties and Other Verses (1886)
Barrack Room Ballads (1889, republished with additions at later times)
The Seven Seas and Further Barrack-Room Ballads (In various editions 1891–96)
The Five Nations (with some new and some reprinted and revised poems, 1903)
Twenty-two original 'Historical Poems' (1911)
Songs from Books (1912)
The Years Between (1919)

Posthumous Collections
Rudyard Kipling's Verse: Definitive edition
A Choice of Kipling's Verse, edited by T.S. Eliot

In addition Kipling wrote and published many hundreds of poems too numerous to include here.